"I'll shoot you."

The words weren't really clear. He frowned, realizing her teeth were chattering like castanets. He knew shock when he saw it. Will felt something like exhilaration, because she almost had to be from the downed plane. A survivor, by damn. Although why hadn't she stayed with the wreckage?

"Please don't," he said quietly. "I don't mean you any harm. I was on the summit of Elephant Butte—" he nodded toward the mountain, not sure gesturing with his hands was a good idea right now "—and I saw a small plane crash. I thought I might be able to help."

She studied him, shaking and wild-eyed. "I won't—" chatter "—let you kill me."

Stunned, Will stared at her. "Why would you think—" And then, damn, he got it. "You think the crash wasn't an accident," he said slowly.

"I know it wasn't." The barrel of the gun had been sagging, but now she hoisted it again. "I knew somebody would come looking for me."

BRACE FOR IMPACT

USA TODAY Bestselling Author
JANICE KAY JOHNSON

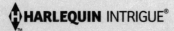

In memory of my dad, a noted Northwest mountain climber
with many first ascents who shared his love of the mountains
and wilderness with his children.

ISBN-13: 978-1-335-13625-1

Brace for Impact

Copyright © 2019 by Janice Kay Johnson

Recycling programs
for this product may
not exist in your area.

Printed in U.S.A.

™ www.Harlequin.com

An author of more than ninety books for children and adults with more than seventy-five for Harlequin, **Janice Kay Johnson** writes about love and family, and pens books of gripping romantic suspense. A *USA TODAY* bestselling author and an eight-time finalist for the Romance Writers of America RITA® Award, she won a RITA® Award in 2008. A former librarian, Janice raised two daughters in a small town north of Seattle, Washington.

Books by Janice Kay Johnson

Harlequin Intrigue

Hide the Child
Trusting the Sheriff
Within Range
Brace for Impact

Harlequin Superromance

A Hometown Boy
Anything for Her
Where It May Lead
From This Day On
One Frosty Night
More Than Neighbors
Because of a Girl
A Mother's Claim
Plain Refuge
Her Amish Protectors
The Hero's Redemption
Back Against the Wall

Brothers, Strangers

The Closer He Gets
The Baby He Wanted

The Mysteries of Angel Butte

Bringing Maddie Home
Everywhere She Goes
All a Man Is
Cop by Her Side
This Good Man

Visit the Author Profile page at Harlequin.com.

CAST OF CHARACTERS

Maddy Kane—Witness to a murder, Maddy has spent a year in hiding under the protection of the US Marshals Service. With the trial approaching, she thinks her purgatory is almost over—until the small plane she's in is brought down by a bomb. Injured, she finds herself deep in the rugged north Cascade mountains and very alone.

Will Gannon—A former army medic, Will is mountain climbing when he sees a small plane go down. He finds a terrified, badly injured woman who says someone is out to get her. Head injury, or truth? Either way, he'll do whatever he must to get Maddy safely out of the wilderness.

Brian Torkelson—Nominated for a prestigious federal judgeship, he can't afford any hint of scandal. Easy solution: Maddy Kane must die.

US Marshal Scott Rankin—Maddy's "handler," Scott has always known he'd give his life for her. In the end, the best he can do is provide the name of the one man he trusts.

US Marshal Robert Ruzinski—Getting Maddy into the courtroom to testify is a frightening challenge, given that the marshals service has been compromised. If Torkelson knew Maddy would be on that small plane, what else does he know?

Chapter One

"This?" Maddy Kane balked like a horse that had gotten a good look at the rattlesnake coiled in the middle of the trail. Her feet said, *uh-uh. No way.* The rest of her was in complete agreement. "We're flying to the other side of the state in *this*?"

She'd vaguely noticed the airfield when she drove by and realized it was puny. Somehow she hadn't translated that into puny airplane.

Having lived in the small and remote town of Republic in eastern Washington the past year, she hadn't expected to board a Boeing 767 here, with only the one short runway and a few hangars by Lake Curlew. But considering she'd never flown in anything smaller than a 737—she thought that was the Boeing company's smallest plane—this Cessna didn't look much bigger than the really terrifying ultralight she'd seen once buzzing over a tulip field, the pilot sitting in what looked like a lawn chair beneath the wings.

Okay, this plane did have a cabin. Still.

The man next to her laughed, the skin beside

his eyes crinkling. A United States marshal, Scott Rankin had been her handler throughout her ordeal. Really, her anchor. As horrific as witnessing the murder had been, thinking the killer would see her huddled only a few feet away, she'd never imagined the fallout after calling 911 and telling the detective everything she'd seen and heard. It had now been twelve months since she'd talked to her parents or sister or friends or the man she'd been dating. Supposedly, her law firm was saving her job, but she had to wonder. A year shouldn't seem so long, but she'd increasingly felt a kinship with Rip Van Winkle. In all these months she'd clung to the knowledge that Rankin was there, a telephone call away.

Graying but still broad-shouldered and strong in his fifties, he had shown her pictures of his wife, adult children and a new granddaughter. He'd been really kind to her. In turn, she'd cooperated with his arrangements. Until now.

How could he think this was the safest way to get her to Seattle, where she was scheduled to testify in a major trial that would begin ten days from now? *Safe* being a relative concept. So okay, flying commercial wasn't an option from this part of the state, but until he knocked on her door this morning, she'd assumed they would drive.

That was the moment he'd said cheerfully, "Nope, we're catching a flight."

Maddy had envisioned at least the kind of twin-engine passenger plane that carried twenty or thirty people. For one thing…there was a mountain range separating eastern and western Washington. A tall one.

She was already toting her bag when Rankin started across the pavement toward the little plane. "Come on," he said over his shoulder, "this'll be fun."

Oh, Lord. For a minute she stood there breathing too fast, until she realized she didn't have an option.

Reluctantly, she trailed him.

Another man had been circling the Cessna, doing what she assumed was a flight check, which ought to reassure her. That meant he was safety conscious, right?

"I don't really like heights," she mumbled to Marshal Rankin's back.

The tall, lanky man doing the flight check straightened and, beaming at them, extended his hand. "Couldn't get better weather for the flight!" he assured Maddy and Rankin.

Sure. By the first day of July in this part of the state, *every* day was sunny and hot. Didn't mean there wouldn't be a lightning storm over the Cascades. A white-hot bolt from on high, and that little tin can would be zapped.

"You'll be able to get a good look at the Cascades," the pilot enthused as if he hadn't noticed her severe case of doubt. "Bird's-eye view."

Maddy squared her shoulders. This was happening, whether she liked it or not. And really, what did she have to fear, compared to the ten minutes when she'd had only a half-open bathroom door between her and a hit man who'd just murdered her new client? This was nothing; people flew in small planes all the time. A lot of people enjoyed it.

The pilot looked familiar, as most locals did. She didn't remember ever hearing his name, though.

When they shook, he introduced himself. "Bill Potter. You must be Cassie Davis. I know I've seen you around. And Mr. Rankin, I assume?"

"That's right," the man at her side agreed. "As I told you, Cassie is my niece. You'll have to excuse her anxiety. I saved the news that we were flying to be a surprise. A drive over one of the passes just isn't the same."

Until she stepped into that courtroom, she would remain Cassie Davis, divorced bookkeeper, instead of Madeline Kane, never-married attorney-at-law. Supposedly, she and "Uncle" Scott were heading for a family reunion in Everett, a city only half an hour north of Seattle. She hadn't asked where she'd be staying. All she knew was that Rankin intended to keep her away from the courthouse until she absolutely had to show. She'd made it through the year in hiding; now she had to remain alive the last few days until she could testify.

The pilot lowered the big door on the hangar and locked it, loaded the two duffel bags in the rear of the plane, then asked her to sit in the back, Rankin in front beside him. "Got to balance our weight," he explained. Either he was really good at faking it, or he suffered from chronic good humor.

Or, heck, he loved to fly this plane and was brimming with excitement.

And she was being a crank.

So she smiled at him before she crawled over the front seat and buckled herself in, per instructions.

"This is a Cessna Skyhawk," Bill told her. "One of the safest planes you could fly in." He had been teaching lessons for something like the past thirty years in this and an earlier model of the Skyhawk, he added, while also offering charter flights.

She held on tight to the seat belt with one hand and the seat itself with the other as he taxied down the runway and the plane lifted into the air. He banked over Republic so she could get a good look at it, he told her over his shoulder.

Despite her queasiness, Maddy did gaze through the window at the town. People had been good to her here. It wasn't their fault she'd felt incredibly isolated. Living under an assumed name, she could never be honest with anyone about who she was or what life she'd actually lived. That meant being friendly without ever really making a friend. Still… as time passed, she'd felt safe.

Stepping into that courtroom, on the other hand, would be the equivalent of confronting a wounded grizzly.

"You okay back there?" Rankin swiveled in his seat beside the pilot and still had to raise his voice to be heard over the engine noise.

She summoned another smile. "I'm good." And… maybe it was even true, because as the plane leveled off, her anxiety lowered. If she didn't look out the window, she could pretend she was on a bus, say. That worked.

As a result she spent the first half hour brooding about the upcoming trial—and then the gap of time between the two trials. Rankin hadn't said anything about those weeks, except that she wouldn't be returning to Republic. Of course, she also couldn't resume her real life until both the hit man and the Superior Court judge who'd hired him had been convicted.

First thing to face was being "prepared" by the prosecutors. As if she hadn't prepped her share of witnesses for trial. Of course, her perspective as a defense attorney wasn't quite the same.

The buzz of the engine at last lulled her into letting go of the troubles that still lay ahead. The pilot yelled over his shoulder to tell her they were flying over the Okanogan National Forest, and would shortly cross the Pasayten Wilderness. She vaguely knew that it took in a swath of the drier eastern side of the Cascade Mountain range. Now she did look out the small window, seeing that sagebrush and juniper hills had been replaced with what she thought were lodgepole and ponderosa pine forest.

She gaped when she set eyes on the first pointy, white-topped mountains ahead.

Bill called out the names as they neared: Mount Carru, Blackcap Peak, Robinson Mountain. Maddy pressed her nose to the small window to see better. She was astonished by the amount of snow, given that this was July. Her awe grew as the snowcapped peaks became increasingly jagged, gleaming white in the sunlight. She could just make out deep cuts clothed in dark green between mountains. A long body of water had to be Ross Lake behind its dam. They flew low enough she could see the oddly opaque turquoise color of the water.

She flattened a hand on the cold window and stared in fascination. Ahead lay a range of mountains that made her think of a shark's teeth. And yes, in the distance was Mount Baker, a conical volcano like Mount Rainier, and Glacier, another volcano. How could she have grown up as close as Seattle and never visited these wonders? Even Washington's most famous volcano, Mount Rainier, seemed mostly unreal, floating in sight of Seattle. She'd never once taken a sunny summer day to drive up to Paradise and see the avalanche lilies in bloom.

She glanced at the marshal to see that he was watching her and smiling.

"This really is something, isn't it?"

"Yes!" It occurred to her belatedly that he might genuinely have been trying to give her a treat.

Oh, and the skinny lake below was called Diablo, according to the pilot, formed by a dam on the Skagit River. It, too, was that startling turquoise color. Over his shoulder, the pilot told her the coloration was the result of the powder from boulders that glaciers ground down. Ultimately, the glacial "flour" washed down the many creeks into the lakes.

They went right over the top of a mountain that was impressive enough, if not jagged like the ones ahead. Those made up the Picket Range, he told her, mountains that had names like Terror, Fury and Challenger, and for a good reason, from the looks of them. The deep valleys between had precipitous drops from the heights, trees clinging to the rocky walls. It was a wilderness that looked as forbidding as the Himalayas or the dense Amazon jungle.

Trying to drink in the beauty not so far below them, Maddy heard the murmur of the two men's voices but didn't try to make out what they were saying. She couldn't seem to tear her eyes off those particularly daunting peaks ahead.

A sudden hard *bang* made the whole airplane shudder. Fear electrified her nerve endings. It felt like a huge rock had struck them, but that couldn't be what had happened.

Clenching her seat belt and the edge of the seat, Maddy looked at the pilot, hoping to be reassured. In her oblique view, he radiated tension. But it wasn't he who riveted her horrified gaze. No, she fixated on the propeller as its blurring speed slowed, slowed... until it quit spinning altogether.

Before that moment of sudden silence, Maddy had never actually heard the thunder of her heartbeat before.

WILL GANNON HAD reached the summit a good ten minutes before, and still he turned in a slow circle to take in the most incredible panorama he'd ever seen. The Picket Range felt close enough to touch and menacing at the same time. One ice- and glacier-crusted spire after another. Mount Baker beyond, and was that a glimpse of Mount Shuksan? Mount Challenger to the north, Eldorado and Mount Logan to the southeast. Rocky ridges, plunging chasms, a sky so blue it hurt his eyes. And quiet. Most of all, he drank in the quiet and the solitude.

He'd chosen Elephant Butte to climb not because it was the best known of North Cascade peaks, or a mountaineering challenge, but rather because most climbers bypassed it. Even on a weekend like this, he could be alone. Later in the summer he might try to find someone who'd like to join him tackling a couple of the more impressive mountains, the ones he'd be foolish to climb alone, but right now what he needed was to pull himself together. After being severely wounded in an ambush in Afghanistan, he'd been shipped back to the States. Being a stubborn bastard, he'd been able to rehab physically. The crap he felt, that was something else. But this…*this* was what he'd needed. Peace and quiet. The vast beauty of nature.

He shook himself and returned to his pack, where he dug out the makings for the simplest of lunches: peanuts, beef jerky and a candy bar, all washed down with treated water. As pure as the sparkling streams looked and tasted, the water wasn't safe to drink without being purified.

He let his mind empty as the sun warmed his up-turned face. Nights when he had trouble sleeping he could remember this. Replace ugly memories of gushing blood, missing arms or legs, sharp pieces of metal thrust like knives into bellies and chests and even faces or throats.

And crap, there he went again. He discovered that he'd closed his eyes, but he opened them again, looked at the spectacular scenery, heard the shrill whistle of what he thought might be a pika, a small mammal that lived among the rocks. It was answered by another, and Will blew out a breath. He was okay. This climb had been a good idea. He'd get out in the wilderness often until snow closed it to him, unless he wanted to learn to snowshoe.

Hey, maybe.

The time had come for him to decide whether to go back the way he'd come, the standard route along Stetattle ridge, or try a different and probably more difficult route. Will leaned toward the different route out of the backcountry. He wasn't in any hurry. He'd brought plenty of food if he ended up taking an extra day or even two, and if he hadn't, he could fill himself with the sweet blueberries ripe on low-growing shrubs at a certain altitude.

Reluctantly, he heaved his pack onto his back and adjusted the weight. Ice ax in hand, he started to pick his way across a patch of snow that began the slow descent. Far below amid a subalpine area of stunted trees and a bright patch of blooming heather, movement caught his eye and he paused. Was he about to have company? Damn, he hoped not. He wanted this day, this mountain, to himself.

Then he identified the patch of cinnamon-brown as a black bear, probably dining on blueberries, too. Not alone. He shifted his binoculars to see her cub. Smiling, he watched for a few minutes, glad his path wouldn't lead him too near to them. Getting between mama and her cub wouldn't be smart.

He'd let the binoculars fall and started forward again when he heard a faint sound that had him turning his head. A growl…no, a hum? It took him a minute to spot the small plane that must have come over Ross Lake and now passed north of Sourdough Lake. In fact, it was heading pretty well directly toward him, which disturbed him on a subliminal level—made him want to sprint to take cover.

He saw the moment the bear swung her head, too, in search of the source of that alien noise. A sudden sharp *bang*, although muted by distance, shot adrenaline through his body. What in hell…? Will lifted his binoculars again, this time to the plane, adjusting until he could all but see the pilot's face. Had the guy dropped some kind of load? Not the best country for retrieval, if so.

Frowning, he cocked his head and listened hard. No more irritating buzz. Oh, crap. The engine had shut down; the propeller no longer turned. The nose dropped. That plane was heading down. He watched in horror as it descended precipitously toward the steep, forested slopes beneath him.

"Start the damn engine. There's still time. Start it!" he shouted.

Following along with his binoculars, he saw the moment the plane hit the first treetops. Cartwheeled. Tore apart.

It might not be safe or smart, but the next thing he knew, he was running.

TAT-A-TAT, TAT-A-TAT, TAT-A-TAT.

Maddy tried to understand the staccato series of rapping sounds followed by silence, then a repeat. Strangely reluctant to open her eyes, she listened hard.

A harsh call. A trilling.

Something brushed her face. She jerked, and pain racked her body.

Have to see, have to see. Somehow she knew she really didn't *want* to know what had happened, but… even aside from the pain, so diffused she wasn't sure what the source of it was, her head felt weird. So she slitted her eyes.

And let out a shocked cry. She was hanging upside down. And looking at a completely unfamiliar landscape. Ground that was tilted. Rocks, the rough boles of trees and feathery sweeps of green branches.

Wanting to retreat into darkness again, she squeezed her eyes shut, but a stern inner voice refused to let her go back into hiding. *Figure out what's wrong. Like why I'm hanging upside down like a bat settling for a snooze.* She'd have giggled if she hadn't known instinctively how much that would hurt.

All right, all right.

This time when she opened her eyes, she lifted her chin to look upward. It took her way longer than it should have to comprehend. A belt across her lap and shoulder held her in a seat anchored to torn metal. *Not a car seat*, she thought, puzzled. Was that…? It was… A wing—an airplane wing—was attached, stabbing toward the ground amidst the greenery.

Airplane seat belt, not car. It was all that held her from falling. A flicker of memory and she knew. *That's why I'm alive*, she thought in shock, trying to imagine the force that had torn the plane into pieces.

The Cessna. In a flood of renewed fear, she listened for voices, cries, *anything* to indicate one or both of the men were alive.

"Scott!" she called. "Bill!" Her "Anyone?" trailed off weakly.

She heard something; she just didn't know what.

Getting down had to come before anything else.

She could open the seat belt, but would drop what had to be eight or ten feet onto her head. Even fuzzy-minded as she was, she knew that wouldn't be smart.

She tried to pull herself upward, grabbing a piece of the wreckage. Metal groaned, shifted, and Maddy froze. Her head swam, and she looked to see bright red blood running down her arm. She must have sliced her palm open. In the greater scheme of things, it didn't seem important. Being fuzzy insulated her. She found a more solid handhold—the side of the cabin, minus the window—took a deep breath and unsnapped the belt.

Her bloody hand slipped from the wreckage and she fell sooner than she'd planned, twisting to land hard on her butt and side. She skidded, bumping to a stop against a boulder. Pain engulfed her and she gritted her teeth against the need to scream.

When she was finally able to move, she wasn't sure she hadn't lost consciousness again. From the angle of the sun through the trees, it hadn't been long, though. Unless she'd lost an entire day? No, the blood on her hand and arm still looked fresh.

Sitting up proved to be an agonizing effort. The left side of her body must have taken the brunt of the damage. Either her arm was broken, or dislocated. Or it could be her collarbone, she supposed. And ribs, and hip. But when she ordered her feet to waggle, they did, and when she experimentally bent her knees, doing so didn't make her want to pass out.

Maddy continued to evaluate her condition. She had to wipe blood away from her eyes, which suggested a gash or blow up there somewhere. Her head hurt fiercely, making it hard to think. And yes, she had definitely slashed open her palm, although she was already so bloody, she could hardly tell where this stream was coming from. None of the blood fountained, though, just trickled and left smears, so she wasn't bleeding to death.

Or dying at all. She didn't think.

With her right hand she clutched the thin bole of a wispy, small evergreen of some kind and used it to pull herself to her feet. Then she turned slowly in search of the rest of the plane. Not the tail—she didn't care about the tail. The nose. The front seats, the two men. Logically, they had to be…somewhere in front of her.

Tat-a-tat, tat-a-tat, tat-a-tat.

Woodpecker, she understood. It kept tapping as she struggled forward, the sound weirdly comforting. Something else was alive, going about its business.

She glimpsed red and white between the trees,

and tried to run even on the steep sideways slope. She fell to her knees and slithered downhill until she came up against a tree solid enough to hold her. As she pushed herself up again, an involuntary whimper escaped her. Her eyes stung—whether from blood or tears, Maddy didn't know.

This time she moved more carefully, watching where she put her feet, grabbing branches where she could for support. The rocky side hill didn't support huge trees. Maybe…maybe these had softened the landing.

And torn the plane to shreds, too.

She saw the other wing first. It had slashed raw places in tree trunks and ripped away branches. More metal lay ahead, another thirty or forty feet.

There she found Bill Potter, still in his seat as she'd been, but the way his head lay on his shoulder— Her teeth chattered as she made herself take a closer look. And then she backed away and bent over puking, snot and tears and blood mixing until she had to use the hem of her shirt to wipe her face again.

She called for Scott, listened. Did it again, and this time she heard a cry. *I'm not alone.* Whispering, "Thank you, thank you, thank you," she half crawled in that direction.

When she saw him, crumpled and twisted, her teeth started to chatter again. That couldn't be right. People didn't bend that way.

She had to scramble the last bit, the ground cold and sloping even more steeply here.

His eyes were open when she reached him, but

beneath his tan his face was a color she'd never seen. His lips were almost blue.

"Scott," she whispered, not letting herself look at his lower body.

"Maddy." Her name came out so quietly, she bent close to hear him. Took his hand in hers, but his chilly fingers didn't tighten in response. Something else she didn't want to think about.

"I'll go for help," she said, unable to help crying.

"No." Suddenly, his fingers convulsed like claws, biting into her hand. His eyes held hers with fierce determination. "Not an accident."

That was something she hadn't yet let herself think. Even though she knew, she *knew*, Maddy heard herself saying, "What?"

"Bomb."

Chapter Two

As Maddy clutched his hand, Scott tried to work his mouth. "Can't trust marshals. Only people who knew."

"That you'd gone to get me and how we were getting back?"

"Yes."

"But…"

"Can't stay with plane."

"I won't leave you!"

"Have to." His voice had weakened. Blood bubbled between his lips.

"No—"

"They'll need to be sure you're dead. Someone will be coming." He stared at her with what she sensed took everything he had left. "Take coats, first-aid kit. Food. Run, Maddy."

Her hot tears splattered onto his face. He didn't seem to notice.

"Friend. Marshal. Ruzinski. Robert. Remember."

She had to lip-read now. "Robert Ruzinski," she repeated.

He made a sound that might have been confirmation. His lips moved again. "Trust him."

"Okay. But I can't leave you."

Staring into his eyes, she saw the very second *he* left her. The tight clench of his fingers loosened. When she lifted her hand away, his arm flopped to his side.

He was dead.

She let herself cry for a few minutes before she made herself think through the cotton candy that seemed to fill her head.

Normally, she'd try to figure out whether there was some kind of beacon and how it worked. Or… would the radio still work? But as it was…

Run.

She didn't dare be found. Not yet. She had to hide. Stay alive until she could really think, evaluate her options. Right now she needed to scavenge what she could from the plane, or she wouldn't survive. She'd seen enough snow before the plane came down to know it must still get cold this high up in the mountains. And there might be some food. Something to hold water in. Yes, a first-aid kit.

Would she have phone reception? Maddy didn't remember seeing her purse. It could be anywhere. She'd look, but the phone, even if it was what Scott had called a "burner," would have GPS, wouldn't it? That might not be good.

Warmth, food, water, bandages—those were her needs. And also… She turned her head to the twisted part of Scott Rankin's body. If he carried a gun, she needed to take that.

The idea of groping his body felt like a hideous invasion. He'd want her to, though—she felt sure.

Shivering, Maddy knelt over him.

HE HAD TO be insane.

Will had had plenty of time to think about what he was doing, and how little chance there was that he'd be able to help anyone. People rarely survived that kind of crash. If anyone had miraculously lived, they might get a faster response from an activated beacon than from him. He'd known from the beginning that he'd take hours to reach the crash site.

But what if the plane didn't have a beacon? If the pilot hadn't filed a flight plan?

Straight lines in this country were rarely possible. No trail existed for him to follow. Instead, he'd reluctantly realized he had to drop from his current elevation of 7,380 feet on the summit and head southwest along the side of the ridge leading toward McMillan Spire. He had to stay above the tree line so he'd see the crash site. Then he just had to hope it would be possible to climb down to it.

This was *not* a recommended descent route from Elephant Butte. In fact, from what he'd read, he'd be facing brutal conditions. Chances were good he wouldn't have cell phone coverage once he dropped toward the Torrent Creek and Stettatle Creek drainages. Even as he jogged along a lengthy band of snow, using his ice ax to aid his balance, he debated whether he should call to report what he'd seen. Swearing under his breath, he made himself stop, lower his pack and dig for his cell phone, which of course wasn't easily accessed. He hadn't expected to want it.

And then when he did find it…he had no bars. Will dropped the damn useless thing back into a pocket that he zipped, then shouldered the pack again and set off.

The speed he tried to maintain was a lot faster than was safe.

Even as he thought that, his feet caught crumbling rock and skidded. He slammed the serrated end of the ax into a crack between boulders and felt the wrench on his shoulders as the ax held and one of his booted feet slid over a drop-off.

Swearing, sweating, he made slow, careful movements to get his feet back under him on a too-narrow ledge. The unwieldy pack didn't help; even though he'd eaten some of the food he'd carried in, it probably still weighed seventy pounds or more. Nothing he wasn't familiar with from deployments, but this was a different landscape. The weight shifted his balance, like a pregnant woman's belly shifted hers. He made his cautious and much slower way to another strip of snow, one of many that formed ribbons between stretches of tumbled rock.

Had to come up here alone, didn't ya?

Maybe this wasn't the right plan. He was strong. He thought he could make it back to Diablo by early nightfall, even though he'd taken two days to get up here. He could call 911 or find a ranger station, get a rescue helicopter in the air.

One that wouldn't be able to land in this mountainous landscape, Will reminded himself.

Still, if he ever reached the crash site, odds were he'd find a dead pilot. Given that this was Sunday, he might also find some climbers or hikers who'd been closer and had already reached the site.

He just didn't believe that. This was early in the season in the high mountains. A warm spring had opened the backcountry earlier than usual. A lot of people would have waited for the upcoming Fourth of July weekend. And even though people down at Ross Lake and hiking the Big Beaver Trail had probably seen the plane go overhead, if they paid any attention to it at all once it crossed the ridge, they'd have lost sight before it began to plummet. Climbers up McMillan Spire might have seen it, but they might just as well have not, too. No matter what, he was closer. Will had a bad feeling that, by sheer chance, he might be the only person who'd seen the crash.

He could do more to help survivors than almost anyone, too, although he regretted the limited medical supplies he carried. Still, as an army medic—former army medic—he'd seen and treated more traumatic injuries than most physicians. Death was all too familiar to him, but if there was any chance...

He groaned and kept moving.

IT TOOK MADDY half an hour and a panicky realization of passing time to realize the rear portion of the plane wasn't where she thought it should be. It should have broken off first and thus been behind

where she'd regained consciousness hanging upside
down. Every step hurt. Even the brush of hemlock or
fir needles hurt. If she hadn't been terrified—*Run,
Maddy*—she would have given up. But she couldn't,
in case Marshal Rankin was right.

Holding on to a tree limb to keep from falling
down the slope, she made herself remember when
the plane first hit the treetops. As their trajectory
slowed, she'd felt hope. And then a wing must have
caught, because the entire plane swung around and
then flipped. What came after, she knew only from
seeing two large pieces of what had been a shiny,
well-maintained and loved small plane.

So…other pieces could have been flung in almost
any direction, couldn't they? She'd been lucky to find
the nose of the plane so quickly. What she'd considered logic wasn't logic at all. The tail could have
ended up somewhere *ahead* of the nose, or off to one
side or the other. It wasn't as if chunks of airplane
would have been shed in a straight line.

She paid attention to broken branches and scarred
trunks. Raw scrapes in the gray rock. Her brain kept
latching on to small, mostly meaningless details.
What was that harsh call she kept hearing? Had
the bang really been loud enough to have been a
bomb going off? Could they have, oh, hit a big bird
that fouled the propeller or the engine? No, Scott
would have seen that; he'd been sitting in front,
right beside the pilot. Of course he would. Then she
started to worry about what kind of animals would
be drawn by the smell of blood. Hadn't grizzlies

been reintroduced into the North Cascades? What if the two men's bodies got *eaten*?

If her stomach hadn't already emptied itself, she'd have been down on her knees heaving again.

Even if she had the strength, could she bury Scott and Bill? Find enough rocks to pile on them?

Run, Maddy.

No. She had to leave the two men, as Scott had demanded she do.

Increasingly dazed, she came by pure chance on a duffel bag hanging above her. It took her a while to find a broken limb long enough to poke at it until it fell. She unzipped it and her heart squeezed in relief when she saw her own clothing. She wanted to hug the duffel just because it was familiar. Hers.

Instead, she made herself toss out everything that wasn't immediately useful. Shorts? Sandals? Gone. One pair of extra jeans she kept, because the ones she wore were so torn and bloody. Thin cotton pajama pants could be long underwear. She kept a toothbrush and toothpaste, but ditched shampoo. A shower was not in her immediate future. Socks—she'd need those. And thank goodness she'd brought her hiking boots. She'd almost left them behind, because she hadn't been a hiker until she had to fill long, empty weekends this past year. Now she took the time to sit down, change socks and laboriously lace up the boots with one hand. She wouldn't need her shoes.

She never did find Marshal Rankin's bag, but did finally locate most of the tail section of the plane. Packed in a compartment that hadn't broken open were two blankets, a pair of parkas, hats and gloves, a plastic jug full of water and a tool kit. Best of all was the cache of energy bars. They might have been in here forever, might be stale, but she wouldn't care.

Anxiety continuing to mount with her consciousness of time passing, she stuffed what she thought would be most useful into the duffel bag, finally discarding more clothes in favor of a puffy, too-large parka and the gallon of water. The shovel that unfolded…she couldn't think what she'd use it for, short of digging graves.

At last, she used one of the shirts to make a crude sling for her left arm, then slung the duffel as comfortably as she could—which wasn't comfortable at all—over her right shoulder.

Straightening, she looked around. She couldn't actually see enough through the trees to orient herself at all. Downhill would surely be easiest. She'd be bound to find a stream eventually. All that snow she'd seen from above must be melting, and the water had to go somewhere.

The flaw was that anyone in pursuit would assume she'd choose the easiest route. Which meant… she couldn't.

She'd go up.

HER ONLY CONSOLATION was that she lost sight of any evidence of the plane crash within minutes. Immediately, she began to second-guess herself. Maybe she would have been better off heading toward a lower elevation where the forest grew thicker, the trees taller. How would anyone find her there? She could huddle beneath some undergrowth until…

I die?

Her mind veered away from the bleak thought. She was panting as if she was at the end of an hour-long spin class, and she doubted she'd been on her way ten minutes. Although it might have been longer, or only five minutes. Time blurred. Each foot upward that she managed to haul herself required an enormous effort. She grasped rocks or spindly tree trunks and heaved herself up. A few times she turned to look back, but all she saw were trees and land that plunged sharply up and down. Weren't there supposed to be meadows in the mountains? Lakes?

The duffel bag grew heavier and heavier. Once she permitted herself to stop and take a few sips from the plastic jug and, despite a complete lack of appetite, eat half of an energy bar, hoping it would provide fuel to overcome her increasing lassitude. Her legs wobbled when she pushed herself to her feet again, but she scrambled upward over a rocky outcrop. Even with boot soles that had a deep tread, her feet kept slipping. If she wasn't on rock, roots tripped her. A few times she found herself crossing bands of snow. She felt too exposed in the open, but too tired to make herself go around.

Nothing in her head felt like an actual thought. She would stare at her feet until one of them moved. At her hand until it found a grip. Her world became the next step, and the pain that tore at her body.

Stop. Have to stop.

Another step.

She hardly noticed when her legs crumpled, when she crawled to the closest thing she could call shelter: a fir twisted by some natural calamity so that it grew nearly sidelong to the ground. Maddy squirmed until she felt almost hidden, and then she curled up, shaking.

WILL CONTINUED TO scramble along among the clusters of the highest, cold-stunted firs. He continuously scanned the trees downslope for any sign of recent scarring. He didn't have to pull out his GPS or compass; he could see over to a facing ridge, beyond which he knew was the deep drop-off into the Torrent Creek gorge. Ahead, water flung itself in a long series of waterfalls. Somewhere in his pack he had a map that would probably tell him what that stream was called.

He did pause now and again to check his watch, dismayed to see that several hours had already passed, and to use his binoculars to scan in a semi-circle.

It was through the binoculars that he saw something off. An animal, maybe, but he didn't think so. The branches of a particularly oddly shaped alpine fir shook. There seemed to be a black lump, and a splotch of red. Part of the plane?

He altered his path with a specific goal now. The descent was damned steep, in places close to a class-three pitch. If he fell…no, he wouldn't even consider the possibility.

The closer he came, the less convinced he was that he'd seen a piece of metal. Somebody might have stowed a pack there with the intention of coming back for it—although this wasn't anyplace logical for a climber to pass through.

He was close when his feet skidded and he slid ten feet on his ass, swearing the entire way even as he employed his ice ax to slow the plunge enough to keep him from colliding with the boulder that lay ahead.

The tree shook. He regained his footing close enough to it to see that a woman huddled beneath the skimpy branches…and that she held a big black handgun in trembling hands. Aimed at him.

Will didn't move, barely breathed as he eyed the black hole down the barrel. "Would you mind pointing that away from me?" he asked.

It wasn't just her hands or the tree branches that shook. It was her whole body. He saw blood, a lot of it, and that she held the gun strangely, the butt almost against her sternum and resting on her other hand—which extended from flowery fabric wrapped around it. Brown hair formed a shrub around her face, poking out in places, matted with blood in others. Her face was a pasty white where it wasn't bloody. He wasn't close enough to see her eyes.

"You're hurt." He did his best to sound calm, even gentle. "Will you let me help?"

"I'll shoot you."

The words weren't really clear. He frowned, realizing her teeth were chattering like castanets. He knew shock when he saw it. Will felt something like exhilaration, because she almost had to be from the downed plane. A survivor, by damn. Although why hadn't she stayed with the wreckage?

"Please don't," he said quietly. "I don't mean you any harm. I was on the summit of Elephant Butte—" he nodded toward the mountain, not sure gesturing with his hands was a good idea right now "—and I saw a small plane crash. I thought I might be able to help."

She studied him, shaking and wild-eyed. "I won't—" chatter "—let you kill me."

Stunned, Will stared at her. "Why would you think—" And then, damn, he got it. "You think the crash wasn't an accident," he said slowly.

"I know it wasn't." The barrel of the gun had been sagging, but now she hoisted it again. "I knew somebody would come looking for me."

"That somebody isn't me. I'm a medic. I'm here in case somebody was injured." Will hesitated. "Can I set my pack down?"

After a discernible pause, she said in a gruff voice, "Okay."

He kept his movements slow. Lowered the pack to the hillside, laid the ice ax beside it and then squatted to make himself less alarming. He was a big guy, tall and broad enough to scare any woman alone in an alley—or on the side of a mountain. The two days of dark scruff on his jaw probably didn't help, either, or the fact that his face wasn't pretty at the best of times.

"Will you tell me what happened? Why you're scared?"

"Who—" mumble "—you?"

"Me? Ah, my name is Will Gannon. I got out of the military ten months ago, after getting hurt pretty bad." He hesitated. "I was shot, so you'll excuse me if I don't love seeing that gun pointing at me."

She looked down as if forgetting she held it. He hadn't forgotten for a second, given the way she was trembling. He hoped the trigger wasn't extra sensitive.

"Oh." She lowered the gun so it lay on her thigh, pointing off toward the southwest. "Sorry."

"Thank you." What could he say that would reassure her? "You're worrying me. I think you're in shock, and I can tell you've been hurt. I have some first-aid supplies in my pack, and I was a medic in the army."

"You promise?"

"Cross my heart." He cleared his throat, recalling the follow-up: *and hope to die.* Maybe not the best choice of words.

But she nodded. "Okay."

He took the chance to rise to his feet, pick up his pack and cautiously approach her. This time when he squatted, he was able to tip her face up and to the side so he could see an ugly gash running into her hair.

"Headache?"

"Yes."

Worse, her hazel eyes were glassy. On the good news front, she was conscious and coherent.

"You mind?" he said, closing his hand around the gun and easing it away from her. A Glock, which meant no safety. Not reassuring given that he'd have to carry it somewhere as he scrambled and fell down into the valley.

That worry could wait.

He kept talking to her as he unzipped the compartment on the outside of the pack that held what medical supplies he carried. First, he pulled out a package of sterile wipes. Once again gripping her chin, he cleaned her face, going through several of the wipes. Antibiotic ointment, gauze pad, tape. Then he asked, "Any other blows to your head?"

"Don't know."

He nodded and carefully explored, sliding his fingers beneath her hair and finding a couple of lumps. He'd have been surprised if there weren't any. Then he dug out a wool knit beanie with a fleece lining, and tugged it onto her head. The afternoon still felt warm to him, but she was shaking partly from cold.

"Were you the pilot?" he asked.

For a minute he thought she hadn't heard him, or was just shutting down. But then she said, "No."

"Was he killed?"

"Both dead. I was in the backseat."

"You're sure they're dead?"

A shudder rattled her. Her head bobbed, just a little.

"All right," he said calmly, "I need to look at your other injuries. Let's wrap something warm around you so you don't get chilled."

While a terrified woman was stripping, he meant. Yep, either that, or he'd be peeling off her clothes.

Chapter Three

Maddy couldn't look away from this stranger she had to trust. As out of it as she'd been, she wouldn't have been able to hold him off for two minutes.

A scar that started at one jutting cheekbone and ran over his temple marred Will Gannon's long, bony face. He had dark hair, shaggy enough to curl around his neck, and he was either growing a beard or just hadn't shaved for a few days. His eyes were light, though; gray or gray blue. Crow's-feet beside them made her wonder how old he was or whether he'd squinted into an awful lot of sunlight. He was tall—really tall, she thought—with the long muscles of a basketball player instead of the bulky, weight lifter kind.

As if his appearance or age mattered. But better to think about him than her situation.

He wanted to inspect all the places where she hurt. Since she hurt all over, was she supposed to take her clothes off?

"Do you…" She cleared her throat. "Do you have some aspirin or something?"

A smile did astonishing things to a face that had scared her at first sight. "I do. But I want to be sure I know about your injuries before I give you anything."

"Oh." If only she wasn't so fuzzy. And cold. "I'm not sure. My shoulder or arm or something. And—" she flapped her good hand toward her torso "—kind of everywhere. Maybe my knee."

"All right. Can I look in your bag?"

She stared at him, puzzled. Without waiting for permission, he unzipped her duffel, sorted through the contents and pulled out a blanket he partly wrapped around her, his enormous hands careful. Then he untied the shirt she'd been using as a sling, and studied her T-shirt.

"You attached to this?"

"What?" She glanced down. "No." Too bad if she had been. It made her shudder to imagine dipping it in a sink filled with cold water. The blood would tint the water red, not just pink.

When she looked up, she saw the knife that had appeared in his hand and shrank back.

"Hey." He waited until her eyes met his. "I need to cut the shirt off you so we don't have to lift your arms. I swear I won't hurt you."

Her teeth chattered a few times before she could get her jaws clamped together, but she nodded and closed her eyes, clutching one edge of the blanket. If he'd meant to kill her, she'd be dead already.

A minute later he said, "Damn."

Her eyes flew open. "Damn?"

"The humerus is broken. Upper arm," he said absently. Fingertips slid along her collarbone, pausing at a sizeable bump she could see when she craned her neck. "Pretty sure the clavicle is, too." He sank back on his heels, obviously thinking. "Let's pack your arm with snow for a little bit before I put a splint on."

He had a splint? Did mountain climbers usually carry things like that, or did he because of his medic training?

He had her lift her right arm, nodded in satisfaction, and explored her rib cage, which even she could see was bruised, and suggested that her ribs might be cracked. "I'll bind them," he told her. "That should make you more comfortable."

A shot of morphine might make her more comfortable. Too bad she doubted he could produce anything like that from his pack.

Instead, he came up with two plastic bags, filled them with snow, wrapped each with what appeared to be one of his T-shirts and had her lie down. Then he placed one snow pack on her upper arm and had her hold it. The other he laid across her rib cage.

"I know you're freezing," he said apologetically. "These will help if you can hold out for a few minutes."

She gave a jerky nod.

He got busy untying her boots, pulling them off and easing her jeans down her legs, too.

She ought to feel self-conscious or unnerved, but she didn't. It was more as if she was standing behind an observation window, watching.

A big purple bruise showed on her kneecap, but

the knee still bent fine and without significant pain. "I fell on my knees a few times," she offered.

One corner of his mouth turned up. "That'd do it. I think it's okay."

That was when she remembered she had a first-aid kit, too. When she told him, he found it in her duffel bag, opened it, grunted and closed it again.

"Nothing really helpful right now." He laid a hand on her calf. "You're cold."

Teeth clenched, she nodded. The heat of his big hand felt so good. She was really sorry when he removed it so he could explore the contents of her duffel more thoroughly. He pulled out the pajama bottoms and clean jeans, then gently dressed her in the two layers. Appearing unsatisfied with the couple of shirts she'd brought, he dug around in his own pack and pulled out a green flannel shirt. It might be way oversize on her, but the fuzzy flannel felt really good when he tugged it on her good side.

Kneeling beside her, he moved the ice on her arm once, finally deciding it was as good as it would get. The splint just looked like a roll of foam to her, but he adjusted it and closed the Velcro fastenings. He frowned when he sat back.

"I should splint your entire arm, but unless you're airlifted, we have to walk out of here. Plus, I don't want the weight of your arm hanging, given the break in the clavicle."

He used the knife on the flower shirt, making a simpler sling that went over the borrowed flannel shirt. Then he rolled the sleeves up half a dozen times, helped her sit up and gave her ibuprofen with water followed by a handful of almonds.

After he tucked the blanket back around her, Maddy saw his expression change, become flat, even hard.

"All right," he said. "You need to tell me what's going on. Why you're scared. And where the wreckage is."

Her fear blasted through that observation glass and was no longer nicely kept at a distance.

She grabbed his arm. "You can't use the radio or the beacon. If you won't promise, I won't tell you where it is."

His eyebrows rose at her challenge. "I found you. I can find it."

Oh, dear God, she thought suddenly. "Have you already called and told anyone what happened?"

His eyes narrowed. They were gray, she'd already decided, clear and occasionally icy. "No," he said after a minute. "No coverage."

Maddy sagged. "A bomb brought the plane down. That's what…" She broke off, trying to think. How much did she have to tell him? Should she still be Cassie or give him her real name? What if he didn't believe a word she said? Not that he was the enemy; he'd been too kind, too gentle and too thorough with her. Still, he might talk to the wrong person. If she started lying now, would he know? Would he be willing to help her get out of this wilderness, just him?

He wouldn't if she lied, that was for sure.

So she took a deep breath, which hurt, of course,

and said, "One of the men with me was a US marshal. He was alive when I found him. He said it had to be a bomb, and that meant he'd been betrayed by someone in his office. Not to trust anyone there. He said somebody would show up to be sure I was dead. And that I should run." Unable to read what this hard-faced stranger was thinking, she finished. "So I did."

And then she held her breath, waiting for him to insist the head injury had made her delusional.

WILL DIDN'T LIKE a single thing she'd said. If she hadn't been so obviously scared out of her skull, he'd have discounted a story so unlikely. Sure, he was climbing in the backcountry of the North Cascades when a bomb took down a plane carrying a now-dead United States marshal and a woman fleeing...who? What?

He muttered something under his breath he hoped she didn't make out and rubbed a hand over his face. He didn't care if he sounded brusque when he said, "You need to tell me everything."

Now she was unhappy, showing the whites of her eyes. Either deciding how much to say or dreaming up lies.

As he waited, he watched every shifting emotion on her pinched face. For the first time it struck him that she might be pretty or even beautiful when she wasn't injured and in shock. So much of her face was banged up, he wasn't sure, but...she did have delicate bone structure and big, haunting eyes, mostly green-gold. Calling them *hazel* didn't do the rich mix of colors justice.

She bit her lip hard enough that he almost protested, but then she started talking.

"My name is Maddy… Madeline Kane. I'm an attorney with Dietrich, McCarr and Brown in Seattle. I was sent to talk to a potential client at her home in Medina. Um, that's on the other side—"

"I know where it is," he interrupted. Medina was a wealthy enclave on the opposite shore of Lake Washington from the city. Was Bill Gates's house there? He couldn't remember for sure, but it wouldn't be out of place.

"While I was there, I had to ask to use her restroom. I wouldn't usually, but—" She shook her head. "It doesn't matter. The thing is, I heard the doorbell ring, and the client let someone in. She screamed. I started to come out just as she said, 'Please, I don't understand.'" Maddy's eyes lost focus as she went somewhere he couldn't go. "She was on the floor, trying to scoot backward. He… I only saw him in profile. He said she was a problem for Brian Torkelson. And then he shot her. Twice. It…was sort of a coughing sound, not very loud."

Suppressor. Tense, Will waited for the rest.

"And he said, 'Problem solved.' He started to turn, but—" She'd begun shivering again. "I stepped back, made it into the bathroom. If he'd walked down the hall—"

Will covered her good hand clutching the blanket to her throat with his hand. "He didn't."

"No." She looked away. "I keep having dreams where I hear his footsteps approaching."

"Yeah." If he sounded gruff, he couldn't help it. "That's natural. I have nightmares, too."

Gratitude showed in her eyes when they met his again. "Do you know who Brian Torkelson is?"

The name rang a bell as if he'd seen it in the news recently. But he had been making an effort since he got out of rehab *not* to follow the news, so he shook his head.

"He's—well, he was—a Superior Court justice here in Washington. Back when this happened, he'd just been appointed to become a federal circuit court judge, which is a big deal."

"But he had some dirty laundry."

"Apparently."

"And you're the only witness."

"Yes. I came very close to being run down in a crosswalk only a few days before Torkelson was arrested. It might have been an accident, but I don't think so. I ended up going into hiding. I've spent the last year in eastern Washington, living under a different name."

"Witness protection."

"I haven't talked to my family or friends in thirteen months. It's been hard, although at least I knew it wasn't forever."

"So Torkelson's trial is coming up."

She shook her head. "Not his. The hit man's." She made a funny, strangled noise. "I can't believe I'm even using that word. But I guess that's what he is.

I sat down with an artist, and the police recognized him right away."

"That can't be enough to convict him."

"The police watched surveillance cameras and those ones at stoplights. I'd gotten to the window to see him drive away. I couldn't see the license plate, but I described the car. It turned out the next-door neighbor had cameras, too. He's a big businessman who's really paranoid. Anyway, once they had a warrant, they got his gun."

"Ah." Hell. "So you'll have to testify in two trials?"

Looking almost numb, she nodded. And that was when she got to the kicker. The dead marshal had told her not to trust anyone in his office except a friend who also served as a US marshal.

"I think I can trust the two detectives I worked with, but word might get out. I'd rather hide until I can talk to Scott's friend."

This was a lot to take in, but Will was reluctantly convinced. "The handgun the marshal's?"

She bobbed her head, although doing so made her wince. "I thought I might need it."

"Have you done any shooting at a range?"

Maddy nibbled on her lower lip again. "No, I've always been kind of anti-gun."

Will's laugh didn't hold much humor. Man, he was lucky she *hadn't* accidentally pulled that trigger.

"Good thing I do know how to use one," he said. "I didn't see any extra magazines in your bag. Did you grab some?"

"No. I didn't think of it. I hated the idea of going through his pockets. It was all I could do to make myself unsnap his holster and take the gun. He had a duffel bag, too, smaller than mine, but I never found it," Maddy concluded.

"All right." Will rose to his feet, not surprised by the stab of pain in his left thigh and hip. It was sharper than usual, probably because he'd climbed a mountain this morning followed by the difficult traverse and downhill scramble to get here. He wasn't done for the day, though, not even close. "We need to move," he said. "I'd like to scavenge anything I can from the plane, and I want you tucked out of sight while I'm doing that."

And verifying the truth of her story, given how wild it was. He didn't really doubt her, but he wasn't good at trusting strangers.

"I thought…here…"

He shook his head. "Nope. I spotted you from a quarter mile away. We need to descend to better tree cover." Her attempt to hide her dismay wasn't very effective. "I'll help. I can carry you if I have to."

Her chin rose. "No. I got here, I can go farther."

BEING THIS HELPLESS was a humiliating experience. To begin with, she couldn't even put her own boots on this time, far less tighten the laces and tie them. Either the pain had caught up with her, or the cushioning shock had begun to wear off.

Oh, heavens—would she be able to lower or pull up her pants when she needed to pee?

Prissy, she scolded herself. Well, she came by it naturally. She loved her parents, but they had been older than her friends' parents, and acted like a much different generation, too. The idea of seeing nature in the rough wouldn't appeal to them, that was for sure.

She tried not to sound stiff when she thanked Will.

When he boosted her to her feet, she thought for a minute she was going to pass out. She tipped forward to lean against him, her forehead pressed to a broad, solid chest.

"Give it time," he murmured, his hand—an enormous hand—clasping her upper arm while his other arm came around her back. Maddy knew he wouldn't let her fall.

Finally, her head quit spinning and she forced herself to straighten, separating from him. "I'm all right."

They both knew that she wasn't, but she'd made it this far and she could keep on doing what she needed to.

"All right." His frowning gaze belied what he'd said. "Tell you what. I'm going to help you down then come back for my pack."

"I can carry mine—"

"Not a chance." He closed a zipper on her duffel and swung it over his shoulder. "Now, which way is the crash site?"

Turning her head, Maddy saw rocks and fir trees—or maybe spruce or hemlock, she didn't know—all set on a precipitous downslope. How on earth had she made it up here? "I…don't know," she said after a minute. "I climbed because I thought anyone who came to the crash site would assume I headed down."

"Good thought," Will agreed.

"I…don't know if I came straight up, or…" She couldn't look at him. His air of competence made her feel more inept. She couldn't even remember where she'd come from. "I'm sorry."

"No." His hand closed gently over hers. "You fell out of the sky. You hit your head and have broken bones. You should be in a hospital getting an MRI. I'm amazed that you were able to get together the supplies you needed and haul yourself up this mountain."

"Is it a mountain?" She started to turn to look upward, but that made her dizzy again.

"Right here, just a ridge, but that way—" he pointed "—is Elephant Butte and beyond it, Luna Peak, and that way, McMillan Spire and… It doesn't matter. Mountains everywhere."

"I saw from the plane." Just before that terrifying *bang*.

"Okay, we need to move."

Maddy wasn't sure she *would* have made it any farther without his help. At moments he braced his big booted feet and lifted her down a steep pitch. Occasionally, Will led her on a short traverse, always the same direction, she noticed, but mostly they picked their way straight down.

The trees became larger, at times cutting off her

view of the sky. Not that she looked. As she had
climbing, she focused on her feet, on the next step
she had to make—and on Will's hand reaching to
steady her. Once they slid fifteen feet or so down a
stretch of loose rocks, Will controlling her descent
as well as he could. Then they went back to using
spindly lower branches to clamber down.

When he stopped, she swayed in place.

"This will do," he said.

Maddy stared dully, taking a minute to see what
he had. The trees weren't quite as stunted as they'd
been above, but were still small. What he was urg-
ing her toward was a pile of boulders that must have
rumbled down the precipitous slope any time from
ten years ago to hundreds. The largest rested against
another big one, framing an opening that wasn't quite
a cave, but was close enough.

Without a word, she crawled inside, awkward as
that was to do without the use of one arm and hand.
By now, she hurt so much she had no idea if this was
doing more damage. Mostly, she was glad to stop—
to crouch like an animal in its burrow until coming
out seemed safer.

Will squatted in front of her, arranging her limbs
to his liking and nudging her duffel bag into place
to serve as a giant pillow.

"I want you to stay low," he told her. "The rocks
will keep you from being seen from above—the air
or the ridge above—but if somebody happens to
come along in the twenty yards or so below you,

they might catch a glimpse. When I get back with my pack, I'll see what I can find to hide the opening."

Maddy nodded. "You'll be able to find me again, won't you?"

His smile changed his face from rough-hewn and fiercely male to warm and even sexy. "I will. I memorized some landmarks."

"Okay."

He reached out unexpectedly to stroke her cheek, really just the brush of his knuckles, before he stood. Two steps, and he was out of sight. She could hear him for a minute or two, no more—and she bit her lip until she tasted blood to keep herself from calling out for him, begging him not to leave her.

She hardly knew him—but somehow she had complete faith that he wouldn't abandon her.

WILL MOVED AS fast as he could. He didn't like leaving Maddy alone at all, but they'd need what he had in his pack. Fortunately, the ascent went smoothly, although his hip and thigh protested like the devil. Still, he swung the familiar weight of the pack onto his back, checked to be sure that they hadn't left so much as a scrap of the packaging that had wrapped the gauze pads, and retraced his steps. Given how he was tiring, he was glad to recover his ice ax to use for support.

This time during the descent he paused several times to scan the forest with his binoculars. Raw wood caught his eye, where it appeared the tops of trees had been sheared off. Yes.

From there, he calculated the route he'd take from Maddy's hiding place. He wished she was farther from the crash site, but still believed her hiding spot to be nearly ideal.

When he reached the rocks, he got hit by a jolt of alarm. What he could see of her face was slack, colorless but for the bruises that seemed muted in color since he left her. Was her head injury worse than he'd thought, and she'd lapsed into unconsciousness?

But then she let out a heavy sigh and crinkled her nose. She shifted a little as if seeking a more comfortable position.

Asleep. She was only asleep, and no wonder after multiple traumas.

She awakened immediately when he touched her, her instinct to shrink from him.

"You all right?"

After a tiny hesitation, she said, "I think so."

"Good. I'm leaving my pack here and going to the crash site after I cut some fir branches to cover the opening. Unless you need to, uh, use the facilities…"

She blinked several times before she understood. "No. I'm fine."

"All right. I'll be back as quick as I can."

Her hand closed on his forearm. "You won't call for help? Or…or let anyone see you?"

"No. I promise." He didn't know what else he could say. It was hard to believe anyone else would show up at the site but another hiker or climber who, like him, had seen the crash and come to help.

Relieved to be unburdened by the pack, Will

sliced off a few branches to disguise the opening in the rocks, then left her. He kept to a horizontal path as much as he could. He hoped the crunch of his boots on the rocky pitch wasn't as loud as it seemed to him. When he paused to listen, all he heard was the distant ripple of one of the streams plunging toward the valley, a soft sough of wind and a few birdcalls.

He'd reached the first trees torn by metal, had seen a white scrap that could be from any part of the plane, when he heard the distinctive sound of an approaching helicopter.

Chapter Four

The roar of the rotor blades was familiar if discordant music to Will's ears. On deployments, he'd spent too much time in the air, often hoping to scoop up wounded men and lift away without being shot down.

He ducked beneath the low-growing branches of a hemlock. Chances were good this would be a search and rescue helicopter arriving at the site in response to a phone call from someone else who saw the plane going down, but Maddy's fear stayed with him. So did the US marshal's prediction. Even aside from Will's promise to her, he wouldn't have made contact no matter who showed up at the site. For now, Maddy had to disappear.

The helicopter remained out of sight, wasn't moving closer. Will needed to see it.

On this sharp incline, approaching without knocking rocks loose to clatter downward wasn't easy. He did his best, knowing the helicopter made enough racket to drown out most other sounds.

He progressed to what he estimated to be fifty yards, spotting other fragments of the plane but not the cabin or wings. Between one step and the next, the black helicopter appeared between trees. With no place to land, it was hovering, as he'd expected.

Will found cover again and lifted his binoculars. From this angle, he was unable to read the FAA required numbers near the tail. He couldn't even be sure they were there. The windshield was tinted, allowing him to see the pilot but not his face. Wearing green-and-tan camouflage, another man crouched in the open door on the side. A rope ran from it toward the ground. The guy turned and seemed to be yelling something to the pilot. Then he lowered himself, swiveled and grasped the rope. Lugging a big-ass pack on his back, he slid down the rope as if he'd done it a thousand times.

Strapped to the pack was a fully automatic machine gun, an AK-47 or the like.

Will had a dizzying moment of seeing double. The other scene had different colors. Vegetation, uniforms, even the painted skin of the helicopter, were shades of tan and brown. At the sight of enemy combatants, adrenaline flooded him and he reached for his own rifle. When his hand found nothing to close on, he blinked. Damn. That hadn't happened in a while. He rubbed his hand over his face hard enough to pull himself back to the here and now. This wasn't Afghanistan, but it seemed to have become a war zone anyway.

He couldn't afford to flip out.

He continued to watch as another man reeled up the rope, waved, and the helicopter rose. It didn't

swing around to head back toward civilization, however; instead, it continued forward, a little higher
above the treetops but low enough to allow the men
on board to search the landscape.

The thing wouldn't pass directly over him, but
near enough. Glad to be wearing a faded green
T-shirt, he pushed into the feathery branches of the
nearest tree and compressed himself behind a rotting stump.

When he was sure the helicopter was receding,
Will held a quick internal debate. Forward or backward? Had to be forward. He needed to know more
about the men who'd been left behind at the wreckage. He had to trust that Maddy would follow his
instructions, and that the pile of fir branches he'd
placed to hide her would look natural from the air.

Two minutes later a raised voice froze him in
place.

"Found the pilot."

Another male voice answered from a greater distance, the words indistinguishable.

So two, at least.

Taking the Glock from the small of his back, he
waited where he was, listening intently. The same
two voices called back and forth. He thought they
might have found the dead marshal, too, but couldn't
be sure. He wanted to do further reconnaissance,
but knew he couldn't risk it. Maddy wouldn't make
it out of the backcountry without him, especially
now that they had to dodge two or more heavily
armed soldiers.

Soldiers? No, they weren't that, he thought grimly. Call them mercenaries. Killers for hire.

The marshal had saved Maddy's life by sending her on the run. Now it was on Will to bring a seriously injured woman to safety despite the men who would soon be hunting them.

MADDY AWAKENED WITH a start, staring upward at raw rock and a crack of blue sky. Completely disoriented, she didn't understand where she was. Pain pulled her from her confusion. Staying utterly still, she strained to listen. Was Will back? But what she heard was far more ominous.

A helicopter.

Her panic switch flipped. Will had sent them to pick her up. He hadn't believed her. He'd betrayed her.

Run.

But he'd promised, and he'd made *her* promise to stay where she was. He hadn't said, 'Whatever you hear,' but that was what he'd meant.

Here, she was hidden. *Stay still. Stay still.* What if they'd captured him, or even killed him? She knew exactly what that looked like. Shivering despite herself, feeling like a coward, she nonetheless refused to believe they'd surprised Will. He'd said he was army. A medic, yes, but didn't they fight, too? Have the same training? She hoped he'd taken the handgun with him. At least he knew how to use it.

The terrifying drone grew louder and louder. Maddy forgot to blink, staring at the thin sliver of blue sky. When darkness slid over it like a shadow, the helicopter was so loud she pressed her good hand to one ear. It thundered in her head, but the streak of blue reappeared and…was the racket diminishing? She thought so.

Did that mean they hadn't taken any notice of the tumble of boulders that had made a cave?

What *had* Will done with the gun? Maddy tried to remember. Before, she'd believed she could shoot someone, and she still thought so. His pack was right there. She groped all the outside pockets but didn't feel anything the right shape. He wouldn't have just dumped it inside, would he? Even so, she unzipped the top and inserted her hand. The first hard thing she found was a plastic case holding first-aid supplies. Packets of what she guessed were food. Clothes—denim and soft knits, something puffy with a slippery outside. A parka. A book?

She gave up, lay back and waited, staring now at the opening she'd crawled through.

Once again time blurred—or maybe it had ever since the crash. Had that really happened today? Was she forgetting a night? Maddy clung to a picture in her mind of Will Gannon, alarmingly tall as he looked down at her. That too-bony face with a nose that didn't seem to quite belong, but eyes that were kinder than she deserved, considering she was holding a gun on him.

Hearing that deep, husky voice saying, *I was shot, so you'll excuse me if I don't love seeing that gun pointing at me.*

The relief of letting it sag, of feeling his big hand close over hers as he deftly took the gun.

Her head throbbed even as the pain radiating from her arm and shoulder worsened.

Please come, Will. Please hurry.

HE STOPPED UNDER cover twenty yards or so from the boulders to use his binoculars again. He could no longer hear the helicopter, but after a slow sweep he found it, deep down in the Stetattle Creek valley. Down there only fools would think they'd see anything from the sky; the Stetattle and Torrent Creeks ran through tangles of vegetation as thick as any jungle. When Will was reading about routes into and out of this wilderness, he'd seen several references to "bushwhacking."

If he could get Maddy down to that low elevation, they'd be hard to find. On the other hand, he didn't have a machete or any other tool that would be good for clearing their way.

He wondered if he wouldn't be able to find something like that in the airplane wreckage. Crap, he wished he'd beaten the damn helicopter there, had time to search.

Couldn't be helped.

He rose and scrambled the distance to the two largest boulders, steadying himself on other large rocks.

"Maddy? It's me."

The silence stretched. He was almost to the opening when she said, "Will?"

"Yeah, I'm coming in."

He parted the pile of fir branches and crawled between them. Same response he'd had earlier. Disliking the cramped space, he wanted to back right out. Tending to claustrophobia, Will had been especially unhappy when his unit was assigned to search caves in Afghanistan for the Taliban. Until today, he'd hoped he would never see a cave again.

Fortunately, this didn't quite qualify.

White-faced and tense, Maddy seemed to be holding herself together by a thread.

"Hey," he said. "You heard the helicopter?"

"It went overhead." She gestured upward. "It blocked the sky."

"Damn." He took her hand in his. "I'm sorry. Ah…hold on. Let me put the branches back in place."

Once he did, he found he could sit up and stretch out his legs if he didn't mind the top of his head grazing rock.

"Did you find the plane?" she asked anxiously.

"Saw a few pieces, but that's all before the helicopter showed up." He couldn't look away from her eyes that were filled with fear. "They didn't see me. The helicopter dropped two men. At least two," he corrected himself. "Only heard two voices. Your marshal was right. These guys look paramilitary and they're armed to the teeth. This was no search and rescue operation. The man I saw was carrying a heavy pack. They're prepared to hunt for you once they don't find your body."

Her eyelashes fluttered. He'd have understood if

she had broken down, but she didn't. All she said was, "What are we going to do?"

"Not get caught," Will said flatly. "This is a vast wilderness. They're naive thinking they *can* track someone. Of course, they'll assume you're on your own, potentially injured, not equipped for such rough conditions."

"They're right."

Had he heard a hint of humor? Maybe.

But she was completely sober when she said, "I'm sorry I got you into this."

"I'm not sorry." Good thing he could be completely honest. "I always liked challenges." Medical school was the one he'd had in mind, not going to war in his own country, but he couldn't wish he hadn't found this woman.

Her smile shook, but it was real. "Thank you."

He smiled, too, and they studied each other openly, he aware of her vivid bruises, the swelling and wild hair, the dirt and scrapes, but also of her delicate beauty beneath. Disconcerted, he knew he had to shut down that kind of awareness. She needed a protector. Period.

"We need to stay here," he said. "At least for the night. The copter is still searching. At some point it'll have to go back to its base, wherever that is. Until it's gone, we can't risk making a move. I want you to rest up anyway. Get some food in you. Your knee might feel better by tomorrow."

"Okay."

Will suspected docility wasn't a normal part of her makeup, but was glad of it for the moment.

"I have a camp stove I can use once it's dark to make a real meal, but you need to eat right now." He dug in an outer pocket where he'd stowed snack food: peanuts, almonds, beef jerky and a bag of caramels.

She wrinkled her nose at the beef jerky, but accepted his water bottle, two ibuprofen and a packet of peanuts. Will found a spot where he could rest his back against a rock wall, and made his own selections for a midafternoon snack. Now that he'd stopped, he was even more aware of the fierce ache in his hip and down his thigh. With a few almonds in his stomach, he downed painkillers, too.

"You're hurt," she said unexpectedly.

"Not that serious."

"You said you were shot."

"Yeah." Will tried not to twitch. He'd done his time in counseling while he was in rehab for physical therapy, too, but he'd never been a big talker. "Just thought I'd take the edge off."

Even as she took a long swallow from the water bottle, her eyes stayed on him, but to his relief she didn't ask any more questions.

How COULD SHE feel so safe in such a strange setting, with a man she hardly knew? Maddy could only be grateful that neither her body nor her subconscious had any reservations about this man. Given the cramped space, they couldn't avoid each other.

The floor of dirt and rock was far from flat, of

course; since it tipped downhill, once she and Will had finished eating, they stretched out side by side with their heads at the top of the slope. Still cold, Maddy wore the parka she'd found in the tail of the plane, while Will wadded his up under their heads. He made sure she wasn't lying on her more damaged left side. They had to do a lot of squirming around until no sharp edge dug into either of their hips or shoulders.

"Use me as a pillow," he suggested, holding out an inviting arm.

As miserably uncomfortable as she was, Maddy took him up on the offer. At first, she lay stiffly beside him, trying to keep some space between their bodies, but he finally exclaimed, "Damn it! Come here." He tugged her closer and gently lifted her arm in the sling and laid it on his chest.

The initial movement hurt, and she cried out, but as soon as she let herself relax, relief washed over her. The weight of her arm no longer tugged at the broken collarbone.

"Better?" he murmured.

"Yes," she admitted. "Thank you."

He made a grumbly sound she took to mean he didn't want her incessantly thanking him, but how could she not?

She tried *not* to think about tomorrow, about more scrambling on this mountainside, whether going up or down—or sideways. Will thought her knee might feel better, but didn't injuries usually hurt more the next day? Stiffen up?

Well, they couldn't stay here, not for long. Even stepping outside this cubby beneath the boulders would leave either of them too exposed. Her worry was how drastically she'd slow their pace. The only positive was that they wouldn't starve to death for a while—there were those energy bars she'd stuffed in her duffel, never mind what Will still had in his pack.

At a funny chirping sound outside, followed by a shrill whistle, she stiffened and raised her head.

"Pika," he said. Since she'd never heard of any such thing, he had to explain that pikas were brown mammals that looked somewhat like a rabbit without the ears and tended to live in rockslides. "They'll have dens down below."

"Like ours."

"Smaller." His voice conveyed a smile.

Sleep tugged at her even as she tried very hard after that to imagine herself home again, and was distressed because she had trouble pulling up faces from her former life.

She woke up enough to notice the light had changed. Of course it had; the sun would have moved across the sky. Okay, really the earth did the moving and the turning, but that was just a technicality. And why was her mind wandering like this?

Because pain was responsible for dragging her out of sleep. Distraction was a form of protection.

Also…she thought her leg might be lying across Will's. In fact, she'd practically climbed onto him.

Embarrassed, she started to shift. The white-hot

stab of pain pulled a deep groan from her throat and had her seeing spots.

"Maddy?" His roughened voice was close to her ear. "You hurting?"

"Yes," she said. "Are we going to run out of pain-killers?"

His "I hope not" failed to reassure her.

"Let me up and I'll get you some. Water and a bite to eat, too." He shifted her as gently as he'd earlier pulled her close, until he was able to sit up and root in his pack. It only took him a minute to produce the water bottle and three capsules.

She gulped them down without asking what she was taking. Without comment, he then handed her a small box of raisins. The sweetness with each mouthful was just right.

"I keep falling asleep," she said. "I never nap!"

"That's an expected symptom of both your injuries and the sheer trauma. You need extra rest to heal."

He had produced a watch at some point, so he was able to tell her it was nearly five o'clock.

She grappled with that. She, Scott Rankin and the pilot had left the small airport near Republic around eight that morning. It couldn't have taken them that long to get deep into the Cascade Mountains. An hour? Two? Of course, she had no idea how long she'd been unconscious, or how long she'd nodded off for when she first hid herself—or now. Still.

She said, "It won't be dark until something like nine."

He raised his eyebrows. "The sun goes down below the mountains long before it's close to sunset."

"Oh." Was that two hours from now? Three? Her bladder was beginning to nudge at her. Could she hold out even that long?

Something else. "Was the bomb on a timer, do you think? If it had gone off earlier..."

"Before you got deep in the mountains." He'd obviously thought about this. "It could have been on a timer, calculated to bring the plane down in the most rugged terrain, or triggered by a radio signal."

"What?" She stared at him. "I didn't see any other planes anywhere near."

"If that's how they did it, they knew the route your pilot planned to take. Although..." He frowned. "Do you know why you were so far north?"

"I think Scott was trying to give me a treat to take my mind off the upcoming trial," she said with difficulty. Having lost him, she realized that she'd come to think of the marshal as a friend. "It worked, too. I was dazzled. Until—"

"Then he must have told someone what he planned. I'd guess somebody was stationed down below to send off a signal once they saw the plane cross over into the most remote and rugged landscape. They could have been in Diablo or someplace along Ross Lake. Could have just pulled off Highway 20 at an overlook and gotten out of the car. No reason anyone would notice someone fiddling with his phone."

"No." She didn't know if it was worse to think

the cold-blooded calculations had been made in advance, or that someone had tipped his head back and watched as the small red-and-white plane buzzed across the sky, then punched a combination of numbers to set off the bomb. He would likely have seen it start to plummet. Had he felt even a grain of conscience, or only satisfaction?

"They brought the plane down too soon," Will said, the set of his jaw hard. "Just a little farther and you'd have come down in the Picket Range. Seems to me, your path was taking you north, maybe toward the pass between Mount Terror and Mount Fury. The view would have been spectacular, and then you could have flown just south of Shuksan. The pilot probably wanted to give you an up-close view of some of the most awe-inspiring country in North America. If you'd hit the side of McMillan Spire or Mount Terror—" He broke off. "I'm not helping, am I?"

She tried to hold herself together. "I want to know. But... I'm not so sure it would have made any difference. The plane was torn to pieces, you know. It was sheer luck that my seat belt held and my section of the cabin got hung up on a tree."

"There wouldn't have been any trees at a higher elevation, say on a glacier. Only rock and ice and snow."

She closed her eyes. "I wanted to bury them. Or cover their bodies with rocks, at least. Leaving them there like that..."

"Was the smart thing to do." Once again he squeezed her hand.

Had Will been as caring with the horrifically injured soldiers he must have helped in Afghanistan or Iran or wherever he'd been? Yes, of course he had. By his standards she was barely banged up. She wasn't gushing blood, hadn't lost a leg or an arm or—an awful picture entered her mind: the grotesquely twisted bodies of the two men who'd also been on that plane.

Something else she shouldn't think about. Later, yes. Not now.

"He knew he was dying," she heard herself say.

"I'm guessing he held on for all he was worth until you found him."

How Will could pitch that deep, almost gravelly voice to be so comforting, she had no idea. Even the expression in his clear gray eyes was a kind of caress.

"He'd have known that if you were alive, your instinct would be to stay with the plane," Will went on. "Maybe activate the beacon, or call for help if you had a phone. He died knowing he'd given you a fighting chance. That would have been important to him, you know."

She ducked her head and nodded at the same time, hoping he didn't hear her sniffling. She'd done a lot of that in their brief acquaintance. He probably thought she was always weepy, which was far from the truth.

"Have you peed yet today?" he asked bluntly.

"How could I? You told me not to move."

He frowned at her. "Then you haven't had enough to drink." He thrust the water bottle at her.

"We'll run out."

"You brought a gallon from the plane. I can treat stream water as we refill both bottles."

Instead of glugging, she sipped. "I thought I should wait until dark to go out."

"Dusk is early here. You don't have to go far."

Maddy hoped she could be as matter-of-fact as he was about the call of nature. So what if he heard her?

"Is the helicopter still around?" she asked.

"I don't think so. I'm sure the men are, but I haven't taken the chance of searching for them with binoculars."

They talked quietly. She drained the bottle; he refilled it from the gallon she'd lugged along with her. Eventually they ran out of impersonal things to talk about. She wanted to know more about him; natural, when she had to trust him, Maddy told herself, but was afraid her curiosity was part of her fascination with this man, a warrior and yet so gentle.

At her question he hesitated but told her he'd enlisted in the army right out of high school. "There was no money for college. It seemed a way out."

"Out?"

He shifted as if uncomfortable to be talking about himself. "I grew up in northern California. Up near Lake Shasta. There's not much money there. Tourism is the only industry, and the people who come mostly camp, maybe want to go out on the lake. We lived in an old trailer." Will fell silent for a minute, lines forming on his forehead. "I don't suppose it was anything like your background."

Maddy wanted to lie but couldn't. What was the point? "No, my mom's a school principal. Dad works at Microsoft. I know I was lucky." More than that, she realized. She'd lived in the protective bubble that privilege gave you until a gunman popped it in an instant.

"Will you go to college now?" she finally asked.

He gazed out at the darkening view across the V-shaped valley. "I got my degree while I served." His shoulders moved. "Part-time when I was in the States, some long-distance."

"You worked a lot harder for it than I did mine, then," Maddy said. "I had it easy." Funny, she'd never thought of it that way before.

He glanced at her briefly but turned his head away before she could meet his eyes. "That's one way to look at it."

The dry way he said that left her with no idea how to respond. He didn't give her a chance anyway.

"I'll take first turn at using the facilities. Then it's your turn," he said, and moved the branches at the entrance enough to crawl out. Despite his purpose, he carried both his binoculars and that ugly black handgun with him.

She couldn't decide if that was more reassuring, or worrisome.

Chapter Five

During his years in the military, Will had learned to set an internal alarm. Awake a couple of hours before dawn, he reluctantly edged out from under a still-sleeping Maddy. Last night he'd shifted the most important things to his pack, stowing non-essentials including extra clothes and the two books he'd brought to join some of what was in her duffel. He'd reluctantly decided to leave the duffel here. He needed a hand free to support her while he used the ice ax to stabilize them.

After lacing up his boots, he had pain pills and water bottle in his hand when he woke her.

Her moan worried him. He'd thought during the night that she radiated too much heat. He'd give a lot to be able to start her on antibiotics.

"Okay, sweetheart," he murmured, "have a bite to eat now."

Uncomplaining, she took the bag of granola he handed her and scooped out a handful. He heard her crunching as he wedged her feet into her boots, made sure her socks were pulled up so no wrinkle would give her a blister, and tightened the laces.

"How's the knee feel?" he asked in a low voice.

She bent and straightened that leg. "Sore," she whispered, "but not like my arm and shoulder."

"Good. When we stop later, I want to apply more antibiotic ointment on your gashes and replace dressings." He laid a hand on her forehead and winced. "I think you have a fever."

Her soft, huffing sound might have been a laugh. "Normally, I'd know because my joints would ache and I'd have a headache, but now…" She moved. Probably a one-shoulder shrug.

Will felt a violent dislike for what he was going to have to put her through. He needed to get her to a hospital, but wasn't so sure he dared even if— once—they reached his Jeep. He thought of a buddy, a doctor, who'd gotten out six months before he did. Javier would probably be willing to call in an antibiotic prescription in Will's name. That was the first essential.

When Maddy said stoutly, "I'm ready," he helped her scoot forward until they were in the open.

The moon had sunk low in the sky, but still cast a silver light across the landscape. That was good in one way, bad in another.

They parted to empty their bladders. By the time she fumbled her way back around the boulder, he'd settled his pack on his back, careful to stow the Glock in an accessible pocket. Not as good as a holster, but the best he could do.

Then they started what would be an agonizingly slow descent of a hillside that had Class-3 pitches—real climbs—here and there. He hoped the men hunting them weren't early risers.

MADDY RELEASED AIR in a slow hiss. How could she possibly do this? But with Will helping support her weight, she skidded down another rocky plunge until she could grab a tree limb.

The sky grew lighter by infinitesimal degrees, from that faintly moon-touched black to a deep gray, allowing her to see the closest trees and where she needed to put her feet next. She swore Will was part mountain goat, the way he picked his way along without dislodging small rocks or slipping. Maddy crunched and skidded on loose rocks, however hard she tried to be quiet. Her knee was both painful and stiff. The rest of her hurt so much that by the time the sky turned pearlescent with dawn she had become an automaton. Her head throbbed viciously, and agony radiated from what must be the break in her collarbone. Probably every movement scraped the broken ends together. Once, she surfaced to realize she'd closed her eyes, her only guidance the big hand on her elbow and an occasional murmur.

"Big step down here." Or, "There's a tree to your right. Grab hold."

Maddy forced her eyes open, feeling immediate alarm at how bright the sky was. The sun would surely be over the ridge in minutes. She and Will couldn't possibly have gotten far yet.

But she lost even that thought beneath the pain. Another step and she'd tell him she had to rest. Yet, somehow she kept her mouth clamped shut so she couldn't beg him to stop. He knew how much she hurt, and why they had to keep moving. A couple of times he'd made quiet, pained sounds after a whimper escaped her.

Maybe she'd rather die. The idea became increasingly enticing. She'd just lie down. It wouldn't be so bad, and Will could go on.

"I won't leave you."

She must have been thinking aloud. God, had she been begging, too, while she thought she was being stoic?

He spoke close to her ear. "We'll reach better tree cover soon. Just hang on, Maddy."

She wished he'd called her sweetheart again. She'd liked that. It sounded…tender.

Gunfire erupted, shocking her out of her dream state.

Will swore, picked her up and plunged downward. They fell onto their butts and rocketed down a drop-off at terrifying speed, ricocheting off small firs. Maddy thought she was screaming, but it didn't matter, did it? Not when the enemy already knew where they were.

They slammed to a stop against a larger tree trunk than any she'd seen. Dazed, Maddy saw Will assessing her before he pulled her to her feet again.

"We have to keep going."

"They're shooting at us."

"Yeah." He half lifted her again with an arm around her waist to lower her over another drop. "They were either out of range, or lousy shots."

The evergreens surrounding them were taller, she realized in what small part of her brain wasn't occupied by fear or agony. Unfortunately, the steep pitch hadn't eased into something a sane human being would consider for a grueling hike.

Will kept her going, the steady pressure of her hand relentless; the hard cast of his face merciless.

Once, she tried to sag to the ground, mumbling, "I can't…"

"You can." His arm felt like an iron bar on her waist as he refused to let her stop, or even slow.

She vaguely became aware that, while still heading downward, the route he'd chosen took them at an angle. Maddy slowly worked out that straight down would have been too obvious.

The sound of running water came from ahead.

"We'll stop here for a few minutes," he said, his grip easing as he lowered her to a seat on a slab of rock.

Maddy stared at the stream, if you could call it that when it looked more like a string of small waterfalls strung together.

"Runoff from the glacier on McMillan Peak." Will pressed something into her hand. A candy bar. He'd already ripped open the wrapper for her.

Once he was satisfied she was eating, he dug out the gallon jug and refilled it, dropping something in—a tablet? He put it away and tore open what she thought might be one of the energy bars from the plane.

"I could have eaten that," she said.

His sharp gaze caught her. "Sugar will give you a lift."

She nodded, not up to arguing. "Are they right behind us?"

"I don't think so. They were firing from well above us. I doubt they were willing to throw themselves down the mountain the way we did. Once we were out of sight, tracking us won't be easy, either. Ground is too rocky." He paused for another bite. "I'm hoping they don't have any backcountry experience. Bringing sleeping bags and freeze-dried meals doesn't mean they're good with rock pitches."

When he saw that she was done with the candy bar, he made her take some swallows from the water bottle. It tasted funny, probably from whatever he'd used to treat it.

Then he unbuttoned her shirt, peeled it off and examined both the splint and the lump on her collarbone that was the furnace forcing pain through all her ducts.

Gently putting her back together, he said, "I'm sorry I had to be so rough. You have a new raw place on your elbow—" he was looking at a tear in the flannel of the shirt as he eased it back on her good arm "—and a lot of new bruises."

"You're bleeding," she heard herself say.

Will glanced dismissively down at the trickle of blood coming from his skinned elbow. "It's nothing." He looked into her eyes. "Can you keep going? I could leave the pack and carry you piggyback."

And cover the same ground twice? Plus, increase the risk of being seen? "No. I can do it."

HE COULD HAVE killed them, throwing them down the mountainside the way he had. Forget bullets. What he'd done was crazy, especially hauling an injured woman along with him. This canyonside had stretches too steep to traverse, never mind descend at a run. What if he'd leaped off a pitch so steep he couldn't control the descent at all?

Eventually, as his pulse slowed and his hands steadied, Will watched Maddy.

People tended to lump together courage and heroism, but they weren't the same thing at all. The person who ran into a burning building to pull someone out often said, "I didn't think about the risks." Heroism was often impulse. Courage, in contrast, could be stoic. It was doing what had to be done, no matter the pain or personal suffering.

He had seen courage to equal Maddy's, but not often.

Reason said they needed to cover as much ground as possible, but when wounded, humans tended to have the same instincts as wild animals. Find a safe place and hide. That was what she'd done initially, and then it had been the best thing she could do. Now, when they needed to move fast, instead of reverting to instinct, she had trusted him absolutely.

Will wished he deserved that trust. Truth was, they'd been damn lucky.

What grated him was that he'd known the bullets were falling short. Sure, they'd needed to open some distance between them and the gunmen, but they hadn't had to take what could have been a suicidal plunge. He hadn't quite flashed back to war, but he'd come too close.

Forget the self-recrimination, he told himself. *Focus*. He had to get them out of this wilderness before the hired killers spotted them again.

After studying his topographical map last night, Will had made the decision to take a southwest path in the general direction of Azure Lake, nestled below McMillan Spire, although he felt sure they were now at a lower elevation than the lake. If he'd taken them east, the drop toward the creek was less precipitous, but he feared it might be more open. With a little more luck, the men hunting them would expect them to go that way. With his chosen route, he and Maddy would have to struggle along Stetattle Creek for a greater distance, but they'd have a better chance of staying hidden in the thickets along the creek than they would on the steep drop from the ridge.

Maddy didn't argue, didn't question him, just stumbled along with his help. By early afternoon, though, she was even slower. Will had a bad feeling she was having to tell herself she could take one more step. That might be all that kept her going.

When she seemed to balk at one point, he turned to find her swaying, her eyes glassy.

They had to stop.

Will looked around. No talus slope, like the one where they'd huddled last night. With the drop in elevation, the fir and hemlock were tall enough to block any view from a distance, however, and an especially thick clump just below them drew him.

"Maddy, we'll spend the night right there." He pointed.

She followed the direction he pointed with a dull gaze, but nodded and managed to take the next step under her own volition.

The trick once they were enclosed in the grove was to find anywhere flat enough to lie down. Reaching for the sky, the trees grew at a sharp angle from the still steep mountainside. He spotted what he thought was a particularly wide trunk but then realized was two trees that had sprouted at nearly the same time and grown together. Dirt and crumbled rock had been dammed up behind the dual trunks. Will used the head of his ice ax to scrape out an area large enough for them both to lie down.

He could have gone on, but was still grateful to lower his pack to the ground, and grimaced at the stab of pain in his hip. When he checked the watch tucked into an outer pocket, he realized they'd started out almost ten hours ago. It was a miracle Maddy had stayed on her feet that long, particularly in such difficult terrain. He was forced to accept how slow their pace would continue to be, too. He could have whacked his way down to Diablo in a day, but with

Maddy… He shook his head. They'd be looking at a minimum of two more days, maybe three, he feared.

As if she had no will left, Maddy had stopped when he stopped, not even sagging to the ground. He hastily spread his thin pad and atop it the sleeping bag, then gently guided her to sit down. Will dug painkillers and water out of his packet.

"Swallow these."

She stared at the three pills in her hand for a long moment before tipping them into her mouth and taking the bottle from him to wash them down.

"That's good. Those will help." He removed the water bottle from her hand and dumped some dried fruit in her palm. "Now eat."

He didn't see any more comprehension when she gazed at the dried banana and pineapple slices, but after a minute she did begin to nibble.

He followed that up with peanuts and more water. A hot meal would be good, but she needed sleep first.

Maddy moaned when he helped her lie down, pillowing her head on his balled-up parka and covering her with the blanket. She still looked so miserable, so he wadded up a sweatshirt under her injured arm, providing extra support.

Startlingly soon, her breathing deepened and evened out, and he saw that she was asleep.

HE TOOK THE chance of leaving her and climbed up to a crag he'd noticed earlier. Lying atop it, Will's view was still partially impeded by forest, but he scanned with his binoculars for any hint of other humans. A red-tailed hawk swooped from above and disappeared into trees. Apparently having decided he was harmless, a chipmunk darted over the rock not five feet from him.

That was it. Will hated not knowing where the enemy was. He'd give a lot for a crackling voice in his ear offering intel, but he and Maddy were completely on their own. *You mean* you're *on your own.* He rejected the voice. She was out of it right now, but all he had to do was remember the way she'd faced him down at first meeting. Despite having survived the crash and suffering significant injuries, she had done a lot of smart things. He hoped like hell that, once she'd had some rest, they would be able to talk.

If her fever continued to mount... He shook off the worry. The same goal remained: get them off this mountainside, through the alder- and willow-choked jungle that protected the stream, to his Jeep parked in Diablo. Even if she was raving out of her head by then, could he risk taking her to a hospital?

Worry about that when it came.

He was trying not to doubt her story. Too much aligned with it, from the plane crash to her possession of a gun she didn't know how to use, and finally to the well-equipped men dropped from the helicopter.

Will thought he could keep her away from them. What scared him was the possibility she'd die from her injuries or a resulting infection before he could get her to safety. But in reality he had no way to call for a rescue helicopter anyway.

Right now he'd feel better to be watching over her.

MADDY SO DIDN'T want to wake up. She squeezed her eyes shut and tried desperately to call back the dream that had thinned like a cloud until it no longer had any substance.

The pain was white-hot.

But her nose twitched, because something smelled good, and despite the fact that her entire body hurt now, she was hungry.

With a groan, she pried open her eyelids, blinking several times before her eyes adjusted to a beam of sunlight that found her between tree limbs.

Just past her feet, Will was bent over the single-burner camp stove he'd used last night to heat water he added to freeze-dried meals. Last night's had been a chicken and rice curry, which had tasted wonderful. Or, at least, like real food. Tonight...

"Stew?" she guessed, her voice croaking.

He lifted his head and smiled. "Yep. I was about to wake you up."

"My stomach did it for you." She started the awkward process of sitting up.

Will immediately rose and offered his hand. As he tugged her up, she bit back a whimper.

"Why am I getting worse instead of better?" she exclaimed. "I hurt all over now. Even my stomach, but especially my legs and feet."

"You do have cracked or broken ribs," he reminded her. Then he grinned. "We started out at four this morning and didn't stop except for the one brief break until two. You know it's harder on the legs to go down than up."

She narrowed her eyes. "Are you telling me I'm sore because I'm in such lousy shape?"

Another grin flashed, making that bony, scarred face momentarily charming and sexy. "I'd never put it that way."

She wrinkled her nose, even though he was right. Even this past year when she'd taken up hiking, her two or three mile outings were more strolls than anything strenuous. She'd probably been more fit before, when she made herself go to the health club at least three days a week.

Smile lingering, Will handed her a pouch and spoon. "Fine dining."

"I'm starved," she admitted, and started eating. She was vaguely aware he was doing the same.

"How's your head?" he asked suddenly.

"Well, I have a headache, but…" It wasn't easy to separate out how her head alone felt. "It's better, I think." If only her thighs weren't screaming.

His relaxation was so subtle, she guessed he hadn't wanted her to know quite how worried he'd been.

"Does that mean I didn't have a concussion?"

"No, I'm sure you did, but apparently not severe. Which is fortunate, given our activities."

Running for their lives.

Maddy frowned. "Isn't it weird that they shot at us?"

"Yeah, I've been thinking about that." He balled up his dinner packet and dropped it into a zip-top plastic bag that held trash. "It's possible that, with high-end binoculars or rifle scopes, they got a good enough look at you to match up with photos. They might have seen the sling and your bruises. Plus, we were in the right vicinity, not that far from the crash site. That said, they had no reason to think there'd be two of us, and we mostly had our backs to them as we descended. They must know there are climbers in the area."

Feeling a chill despite the warmth of the afternoon, Maddy said, "Is it possible that they didn't want anyone who might conceivably have seen the crash site to get out and report it?"

His implacable expression belonged to the soldier he'd been. "That's my bet," he said after a moment. "If rescue personnel showed up and they caught a glimpse of a pair of mercenaries equipped with AK-47s, what're they going to think? And if they locate the crash and find one of the dead men was a US marshal, that would set off a serious hunt for the missing passenger. No, they need to—" He broke off, an apology in his eyes.

"Eliminate me," Maddy finished. "That's what you were going to say, isn't it?"

"And any witnesses."

"The trouble is, now they have to make *you* disappear, too."

His eyebrows climbed. "If you're thinking of apologizing, don't. I was where I needed to be."

How lucky had she been, to have Will Gannon come running to her rescue? A soldier, a medic and a man of honor.

"You'll have to let me thank you eventually."

He grunted. "Wait until we're back to civilization."

Maddy bent her head and finished her dinner. After disposing of the packet and giving him back the metal spoon, she said lightly, "I don't suppose you have any English breakfast tea in that backpack?"

"No, but I have coffee. Like a cup?"

"Are you kidding? I would *love* coffee."

Will laughed. "Won't take long to heat the water."

Two years ago she'd have disdained instant coffee. After all, there were at least two coffee shops on every block in Seattle, and coffee stands in most downtown businesses, too. This was only one of the many ways her life had changed.

In no time he handed over coffee that contained both sugar and creamer. Will sat beside her on the sleeping bag, his cup more a bowl. He'd offered her a choice of two candy bars, too.

"Was it Mary Poppins who could produce amazing things from her carpet bag?" Maddy asked.

The corners of his mouth twitched. "I'm sure I saw the movie, but I mostly remember the umbrella."

She couldn't resist singing, "Just a spoonful of sugar makes the medicine go down. You even had sugar."

Will chuckled. "Fortunately, I overpacked. I thought I might stay an extra couple of days in the backcountry instead of heading right out."

"You're doing that, all right," Maddy murmured. "Only you're having to feed two of us."

The gray eyes resting on her were intent and… warm. "Food may get scanty by the end, but we'll be all right." He smiled. "I'll buy you a burger and fries on our way home."

The thought was lovely, but unreal. It might not be that many miles as the crow flies to the nearest burger joint, but she could barely walk. Still…it was something to hold on to.

"Where do you think those men are?" Maddy heard herself ask. "You don't seem worried."

In fact, Will's pose was casual, one long leg outstretched, the other bent. He hadn't yet hushed her, or kept his voice especially low. She knew the odds were slim that Torkelson's hired gunmen would either be able to track her and Will or happen to stumble on them, given the vast expanse of wilderness, but it wasn't that many hours since they'd been fired on.

All the tension his body didn't give away was in his eyes when they met hers. "It's time I show you where I think they are, and why we have a problem."

He spread out the topographical map, which clearly displayed elevation and how steeply it rose. Never having seen one before, Maddy watched closely as his finger tapped first on the summit of the mountain he'd climbed, then the approximate location of the crash…and finally their current location, at his best guess. And yes, experience with map reading wasn't necessary to see the problem.

Unless they were to do some serious scrambling and pass over a glacier at the foot of the sharp peak of McMillan Spire to descend into a different V-shaped creek valley, there was only one way out. Stetattle Creek.

Will put the obvious into words. "They don't know where we are now. But unless they're stupider than we can count on, they do know where we'll be soon."

Maddy couldn't tear her eyes from the map. "They'll be lying in wait."

Chapter Six

"What if we did go up?" Maddy asked, out of the blue.

It was several hours later, and they'd decided to hit the sack, literally, given that their only bedding was a single sleeping bag and one blanket. Since Will had shown her the map and the hard reality ahead of them, they'd talked about other things, quietly and with no urgency. Nothing important, and yet the experience had been strangely intimate. There'd been no pretense between them, no game playing. Will recognized the experience; nights before his unit was to head into the kind of action some of them might not come out of alive, they'd talked like this.

A sharp-edged memory popped up. Alan Todd had described one night's spare meal and quiet conversation as the last supper. Will wondered later if Todd could have had a premonition. He'd died the next day, only weeks before Will almost bought it.

He shook off the recollection. This wasn't like that—except it was.

He didn't think either he or Maddy had said a

word in nearly an hour now beyond the practical. They'd shared a cup of water to brush their teeth and, in her case, take some more of his dwindling supply of pain meds. He went one way, her another, for a few minutes of necessary privacy. Now, although night hadn't fully darkened the sky, he had sprawled on his back and was helping Maddy arrange herself as comfortably as possible beside and on top of him.

Her softly voiced question followed a few gasps and small cries of pain as she slowly, awkwardly lay down. Will had had a broken collarbone once, and remembered well what the first weeks had been like. Add cracked or broken ribs, and lying down wasn't the relief you'd expect. At least last night they'd figured out the most comfortable position for her.

Once her broken arm lay on his chest and her head nestled on his shoulder, he said baldly, "You're in no condition to go mountain climbing. It could add two days to our trip, and a good part of that would be in the open, above the tree line. What if they're watching? Or the helicopter comes back for a flyover?"

She didn't say anything.

"Stetattle Creek will be hard enough to follow. Terror Creek is notorious. And if we made it, we'd pop out at Newhalem instead of Diablo where I parked my car. I could hide you and hitch a ride, I guess, but if those bastards got a good look at me—"

The way she sucked in a breath, he knew he didn't have to finish.

Truth was, he had enough worries about the Stetattle Creek route. The tangle of vegetation would be bad, and he had no doubt they'd also be swarmed by mosquitoes. They might have to cross back and forth over the creek if and when one bank was especially inhospitable, and how would Maddy do on slippery rocks or trying to edge across a fallen tree trunk? Bullets might come out of nowhere. And then, the last part of the route was on an honest-to-God trail that wasn't heavily used, but was promoted in the couple of guidebooks he'd seen. What would he or Maddy say to strangers met on the trail? Gosh, gee, had a little accident but she's fine? They'd remember her, talk about her in the campground or the store, maybe mention the green Jeep they'd seen the odd couple drive away in.

He and Maddy would not emerge from the wilderness unseen, which presented a danger as real as the ambush he had no doubt they would meet at some point higher up on Stetattle Creek.

Damn, maybe he should rethink this. But it didn't take a moment for him to know he'd made the only possible decision. Her fever hadn't climbed, but she was still too warm, which meant infection was working somewhere in her body. The fact that she'd be miserably sore tomorrow wouldn't help. And then there was the food situation. If all went well, they wouldn't starve to death, but his supply had dwindled alarmingly, and she needed fuel to overcome the pain.

As he lay there looking up, seeing bats darting against the deepening sky, she lay stiff until he lifted his free hand and smoothed her hair from her face, then kept stroking her, fingertips only, and carefully. Temple, cheekbone, the bridge of her nose and the uninjured side of her forehead.

She sighed and snuggled closer. Five minutes later he knew she'd fallen asleep, leaving him alone with his thoughts.

Fears and doubts raced like a hamster on a wheel. At the same time, he was distracted by the soft press of Maddy's breasts, the curve of her hip, the warmth of her breath in the V of his shirt. When was the last time he'd held a woman? Had to be months before he'd come so close to losing his leg or even his life. She—whoever she was—hadn't felt as good as Maddy did.

Funny to think that, considering her hair was still matted, the left side of her face was garishly discolored and swollen and she probably didn't smell sweet. Since he hadn't had more than what his father called a sponge bath in… Will had to think. Damn, had it really been five days? Well, he wasn't going to lift an arm and do a sniff test. He did have a bar of soap and a towel in his pack. Once they reached the creek, they could both clean up. He hadn't brought so much as a comb, but there'd been a brush in her duffel. He hoped he had transferred it to his pack.

You want to die clean?

Irritated by the defeatist voice in his head, he returned to his original thought.

He liked sleeping with Maddy Kane. He'd like to do more than sleep, once every movement didn't cause her pain.

She stirred and gave a small moan. Will smiled wryly, kissed the top of her head and closed his eyes.

MADDY SURFACED TO a gray dawn, the now too-familiar awareness that if she moved it would hurt... and that, once again, she was all but draped over an exceptionally solid male body.

His breathing changed almost as soon as she opened her eyes.

"Morning, sunshine," he said huskily.

"That's me," she mumbled, struggling to remember what day this was. Tuesday, she finally decided.

The muscular wall of his chest vibrated with a laugh. "Speaking of sunshine, doesn't look like we'll have any today."

She'd gotten so used to eastern Washington's drier, sunnier climate, the possibility of gray drizzle startled her. Getting wet was sure to make everything much worse. She didn't comment, however, because they had to move on. Whining was useless.

She did wince when she stretched her legs, hoping they wouldn't cramp. As soon as she was on her feet, she limped stiffly off to pee. When she returned to the camp, she found Will heating water.

He glanced at her with a smile. "I figured we could take the time for coffee."

"Bless you."

He skimmed her with an assessing gaze. "How are you?"

"Sore," she admitted, "but my knee feels better." She hoped that wasn't wishful thinking.

While they ate a hasty breakfast of granola and dried fruit, he told her about the time he'd broken his collarbone in a pickup football game on base. "Fortunately, I wasn't due to be deployed, or my lieutenant would have been seriously unhappy. It gets less painful as it goes, but I'm sorry to tell you it took months to completely heal."

"How does the bone ever knit when it's constantly being shifted?"

"Got me." He added powdered milk to her coffee and handed it over.

"So."

Will looked at her inquiringly.

"How are we going to avoid getting gunned down?"

"By moving slowly and doing reconnaissance."

"And what if they shoot some poor climbers on their way down?"

He shook his head. "This isn't a common route. I think it was Fred Beckey, one of the great northwest mountaineers, who called whacking your way up or down the thickets in these valleys 'pure misery.'"

She digested that. "Are you telling me there's a better way?"

"From where we are now? No. To climb Elephant Butte, I came along the top of Stetattle Ridge from Sourdough Mountain. I could have followed another ridge from there to McMillan Spire. Otherwise, climbers in the southern Pickets sometimes drop down Terror Creek until it meets Goodell Creek, which leads to the Skagit River. That's the way we could have taken if we'd been willing to climb up and over. Stetattle Creek is doable, but not popular. Although I really wonder whether there's any difference."

She only nodded. What was there to say?

Will stared down into his coffee for a disquieting minute, then swallowed what was left and began to pack up.

Within minutes they were ready to go.

They might not have reached the "pure misery" part of the descent, but the still incredibly steep downhill pitch was torment enough for Maddy. She hadn't been on flat ground since the airport by Republic. The trees were now larger than the ones where the plane had come down, but otherwise every step was as difficult. She had to use her good hand to grab whatever branch or rock was available and slither or pick her way a few feet down. Will always descended first then turned to either lend her a hand or be ready to catch her if she fell.

Her arm and chest felt like…she didn't know. Burning embers. With her arm in the sling, it almost felt as if she were carrying the agony in the crook of her arm, something she didn't dare drop.

Her calf muscles and quads weren't happy with her, either. That, at least, was normal. She told herself to pretend she was pushing it on the elliptical in the gym, in those once-upon-a-time days when looking great in Spandex was a big part of her goal. Yes, her muscles had screamed then, but she'd never insisted they keep screaming until they became hoarse.

Every so often she saw a squirrel or a chipmunk, a quick dart, whisk of a tail, bright eyes watching these intruders in their wilderness. Will stopped her once with a hand on her arm.

"Listen."

Tat-a-tat.

"Woodpecker," she whispered. "That's the first thing I heard when I regained consciousness after the crash."

His gaze sharpened. "You were unconscious? For how long?"

"How am I supposed to know? It's not like I was paying attention to time anyway, and then after… my phone was gone."

Tat-a-tat.

"Sorry," he said. He squeezed her hand and started out again.

Until he paused to help her, she could only see his shoulders, the bulk of the pack and those long, strong legs. Lying down, she tended to forget quite how tall he was. At five foot seven, she wasn't short for a woman, but the top of her head barely reached above his shoulders.

Maddy wondered how much he chafed at their halting progress. She imagined him bounding downward—but he'd probably have taken a different route if he hadn't seen her plane go down and saddled himself with the injured survivor. Except she knew he'd meant it when he said, *I was where I needed to be.* Even…where he wanted to be?

As she tired, her thoughts bounced around as if

they were in a pinball machine. What Mrs. Brophy would think when her bookkeeper didn't come back after the two-week "vacation." The view from her small office in the law firm in Seattle, including just the tiniest slice of the water. Her then-boyfriend reaching for her hand instead of Will. For an instant she was confused. Doug got manicures. He had narrow, elegant hands and absolutely no calluses. His hand didn't engulf hers the way Will's did, either.

Doug would have been no help to her at all in the wilderness with killers on her heels.

The word *killer* switched her to a loop she'd rerun thousands of times. The man standing over her terrified client, the big black gun. The *pop*, *pop*. How close Maddy had come to falling back. A face impassive but for a trace of disgust or irritation. The way his head came up suddenly, turned as if he'd heard her breathe, knew suddenly there was someone else in the house. If he'd looked for her, she wouldn't be here now. But then, two good men wouldn't have died horribly because of her, either.

Yes, but she wouldn't have had the chance to put him away for a lifetime, and maybe Torkelson, too. Having betrayed his office, he was almost worse.

"Doing okay?"

Will's voice jerked her from the dark memories.

"Peachy."

The cheek she could see creased with a smile.

Maddy's thoughts blurred as she plodded on.

Midday, she heard a waterfall. Maddy blinked and looked around, suddenly realizing that the vegetation had changed. Deciduous trees—alders? Vine maples?—were mixed with the fir and hemlock. Lacy something draped from tree branches. She took another step and skidded on what she realized was deep green moss covering a rock.

A firm grip on her upper arm kept her upright.

They stopped for a rest, drink of water and bite to eat on a mossy downed log.

"It's going to be really slow going from here on," Will warned her. "We may get lucky and find a few game trails, but mostly we need to stay up above the creek, which is likely one waterfall after another for this first stretch."

Another sound blended with the rush of water. She cocked her head. "What's that?"

"A bird. Maybe a warbler? We'll see more of them, and mammals, too. Deer and black bears are the biggest. Elk tend to stick to marshy land and meadows."

"Bears?"

He smiled. "I saw a mama and her cub eating blueberries before your plane went down. They didn't pay any attention to me."

A branch rustled not far away and Maddy looked in alarm to see a small bird sidling along watching them. It had a creamy-white chest, brownish wings and back, with black circling a yellow crown on its head.

"That's a sparrow, I think," Will said quietly. "There are half a dozen kinds up here."

The bird flew away so fast her eye couldn't follow it.

"The vegetation is going to get thicker," Will continued. "Unfortunately, insects like these conditions, too. Flies and mosquitoes will be the biggest annoyance. I'd like to keep some elevation above the creek for now, which may save us from getting sucked dry, but if we find a pool, we might be able to wash up."

Maddy suddenly felt gross—sweaty, her hair greasy, what bare skin she could see on her forearms dirty and streaked with pitch where dried beads of blood didn't show new scratches. With deep longing, she asked, "You mean, actually get in the water?"

"Ah, probably not that." He leaned to scratch his back on a tree trunk. "This water is melt from the glacier. The temperature won't be much above freezing." A teasing light in his eyes, he added, "Depends on how tough you are."

She wrinkled her nose. "I'd love to get clean. I have to admit, though, that I'm the kind who inches into cold water instead of diving in and getting it over with."

He laughed quietly, stretched and shoved his arms beneath the straps of the backpack. "Ready?"

As they set out again, he said, "Let's keep our voices down."

Maddy nodded, the reminder making her skin prickle with apprehension.

WILL'S BEST GUESS was that the gunmen would be waiting downstream, closer to where Torrent joined

Stetattle Creek, but he couldn't take anything for granted. First chance he saw, he wanted to cross to the other side, both because his topo map suggested the going might be easier and because the men might assume they'd stay on this side.

He stopped Maddy when he saw what he'd wanted: a large tree that had fallen across the stream just below a waterfall.

"Stay here," he said quietly. "Let me take a look around."

He scanned with his binoculars before moving, stopping when movement caught his eye. Identifying a river otter reassured Will. Would it be on the bank if it had seen or smelled humans too close? It obviously hadn't sensed him and Maddy yet.

He handed his binoculars to Maddy, murmuring, "Look right above the boulder across the creek."

She gave an almost soundless gasp when she saw the otter. "Two of them!"

Will took another look. Sure enough. As he watched, one slid back into the stream, followed almost immediately by the other. They hadn't moved as if they were alarmed, though.

He'd believed himself prepared for what they'd find in the V of the valley. Two minutes of trying to ease between tangles of alder growing out of rock changed his mind. Bulling through was probably the right technique, but that wasn't compatible with trying to go unseen. He thought he was doing pretty well until an alder caught his boot and sent him crashing down. As he braced his hands to jump

up, something jabbed his face. Swallowing a pro-
fanity, he glared at the cluster of leaves edged with
spines he recognized from a guidebook. The shrub
was appropriately called devil's club.

He forged on until he reached the torrent of water
bounding down what had once been a talus slope.
When the tree fell, it had ripped its roots out of the
soil. Already, lush vegetation had filled in the hole,
which wasn't visible. An unwary step and he'd have
gone down again. He believed in planning ahead,
but didn't even want to think about what they'd do
if he broke a leg.

Employing his binoculars again, all he spotted
were a few birds. When a swarm of horse- or deer-
flies surrounded him and began biting, Will barely
kept himself from swearing out loud. Swiping them
off with one hand, he backtracked.

Sitting where he'd left her, Maddy didn't try to
hide her relief.

"All clear," he said, "but it's hard going. Take each
step carefully. The damn alders will try to trip you
up, and there's loose rock hidden by devil's club."

Once they started off, he used his ice ax to
point to the first spiny leaves he saw, in this case
on a small shrub. Maddy reached out to touch and
jumped when she found a spine.

"There'll be nettles, too. You'll want to keep your
hand up so you don't brush it."

She nodded vigorously.

This time he separated branches and didn't shift
his weight until he found solid footing. Then he

turned and reached out for Maddy, who picked her way as carefully as he'd asked.

The roar of the falls grew louder in their ears. When the stream came into sight, he pointed out the log and the hidden pit below the mass of earth and roots.

He bent to talk right into her ear. "I'll cross first with the pack, then come back to help you."

She nodded.

Damn, he hoped the log wasn't slippery. They couldn't afford for either of them to fall, and she'd have a hell of a time scooting herself across on her butt with the use of only one working hand and arm.

Right beside the bank Will was able to step up onto the log. He moved one foot, then the other, experimentally. Not too bad. He bounced a little, finding it to be solid. Finally, he started forward cautiously. If crossing a pool, he wouldn't have worried about falling. The drop wasn't that far. Instead, below was a tumble of rocks and white water.

Once he stepped out over the torrent, water from the falls misted him. He had to blink water away. The tree must have fallen this spring, he decided, or it would already be covered by slick green moss. As it was, Will made it over and stowed his pack in a dry place.

He crouched briefly to check that the Glock hadn't slipped too deep in the pocket to be easily available. Then he walked back across the stream with more confidence.

"That doesn't look hard," she said. "I usually have good balance. I even did gymnastics when I was a kid, balance beam included."

He grinned at her. "You mean, you could do a backflip on this thing?"

"No, but once upon a time I could have done a somersault and maybe jumped into a kind of split."

His sense of humor evaporated. "Well, don't."

She gave him an unreadable look, but let him help her climb up onto the log. Having decided to go first, he took her hand and put it on his belt. Satisfied when her fingers curled around it, he started forward.

He glanced over his shoulder a couple of times, worried about whether he'd shortened his stride enough, whether her head injury had affected her balance.

Even as he thought, *Pay attention to keeping your own damn balance*, one of his feet shot out from under him.

He teetered over the tumble of rocks and white water, knowing he'd pull Maddy with him if he fell.

Chapter Seven

Head bent, Maddy concentrated on her feet. This must be harder for Will, she couldn't help thinking, with his much larger feet. He walked with confidence, though, steadying her…until she felt him lurch. Looking up in horror she saw him stagger and flail his arms in a desperate attempt to regain his balance.

"Let go!" he roared.

Instead, she tightened her grip on his belt and leaned the other way as a counterbalance. She didn't let herself think about how much he outweighed her by.

The battle was brief. Swearing, he came upright and she did the same. Her pulse had skyrocketed and she gasped for breath. Neither moved for at least a minute.

When finally his muscles tensed, she felt it. As if nothing had happened, he took the next step. Like an echo, she did the same.

On the other side he hopped off the log and turned to reach for her. Water dripped down a face drawn

tight with strain. His mouth was clamped shut, tur-
bulence in eyes darkened to charcoal.

Hands at her waist, he swung her down but didn't
release her. Instead, he just looked at her. Voice
hoarse, he said, "I'd have taken you with me."

"I...didn't think," she admitted.

He shook his head. "I should say thank you, but
when I think of you falling onto those rocks—"

She shivered at what had been a very real possibility. She didn't like imagining *him* hitting rocks,
his body tossed by jets of white foam. "We're okay."

"Yeah." His hands slid up her back until his arms
closed around her. She let herself lean on him, hear
how hard his heart hammered. After a minute he
murmured, "We're good."

Being so close to him felt good. Necessary.

But he drew a deep breath, let his arms drop and
stepped back. "We need to keep moving."

Even as she regretted the space that had opened
between them and the mask he'd drawn over his
face to hide what he felt, Maddy knew he was right.
She still felt shaky, but that was more likely because her muscles were rebelling against the past
two days' exertions than as a reaction to the near-
disaster, although she wouldn't swear to it. Neither
cause kept her from walking.

Just ahead of her, Will plunged into a dense wall
of greenery. Maddy hurried to follow, suddenly
alarmed. If he got ten feet ahead of her, she'd lose
sight of him.

Over the next ten minutes, as they shoved through

alder thickets, sweated and swatted at insects, Maddy thought of that mountaineer's description: pure misery. And he, at least, hadn't also faced an ambush.

Jerking her hand away, too late, from a clump of nettles, she also envisioned Will's map. It was not encouraging to think, *We've barely started.*

WILL HAD NEVER been happier to see the trace of a game trail. At this point he didn't give a damn what animals used the trail, wearing down some of the low-growing plants and breaking whip-thin alder branches that would otherwise be trying to slap his face. Could be wolves, deer, bears or all of the above. A wealth of mammals made their homes in these mountains, including badgers, pine martens, minks and some of the big cats, which were unlikely to allow themselves to be seen. Like marmots and pikas, bighorn sheep and mountain goats stuck to the higher elevations, and he thought elk preferred marshy lowlands. There were undoubtedly beaver dams along the Stetattle—in fact, if he and Maddy were ever to get their bath, it would probably be in a pool behind a dam built of sticks. Some of those animals were nocturnal, which was just as well. Give him a bear any day over an annoyed porcupine.

Maddy tugged urgently on his shirt. "I hear something behind us."

He didn't waste time swearing. "This way." He urged her into a dense tangle of alder and devil's club.

She moved as fast as she could. When she tripped

on a rotting, downed log, he rescued her from the fall but said, "Get down behind it."

Within seconds both sprawled flat amid ferns and lower branches of a tree with sharp needles. Will withdrew the handgun from the pack and raised his head, expecting to see armed Taliban slipping in near-silence through these woods.

He blinked. Wrong landscape. *Not Taliban.* He was disturbed by an expectation so vivid; the enemy soldiers had momentarily had real substance.

Will watched for any movement.

Like Maddy, he heard the rustling of branches first. Was that a camouflage uniform…? He expelled air in relief.

"Take a look," he whispered. "Quick."

Maddy carefully lifted her head, too. "Ooh."

The doe was followed by two fawns, spotted and with impossibly long, slender legs. Will bet they weren't more than a few weeks old.

"Those creeps wouldn't shoot her, would they?"

"Gunfire would give away their position. It would draw attention they don't want, too. Hunting and guns are illegal in a national park."

Her gaze shifted to the Glock in his hand. He smiled wryly. "Don't blame me."

The sound of her soft chuckle went straight to his groin. He almost groaned. "Can you go on for a while longer?"

Her "Yes" was clipped. Maddy rolled away from him.

Crap. He'd been curt, killing the mood. Just as

well. He couldn't afford to let her get to him. His focus had to be absolute, getting Maddy out of the mountains safely his only goal. Later…

Not later. Never. The gulf between them was too wide, too deep. He'd grown up in poverty, she in privilege. He'd scraped out a BA from community colleges and online courses; she'd gone to Stanford and had a law degree. The men she dated didn't have ugly scars on their faces and bodies. They knew fine wines, the best restaurants, not the layout of cave systems where terrorists had set up camp. Will liked and admired Maddy—yeah, he wanted her, too—but she wasn't for him.

Game trail or not, their pace was painfully slow. They took a break for her to down more pain pills and for them both to eat or drink. He ate some nuts but skipped the candy bar. He hoped she hadn't noticed how few were left. Instead, he gave one to her while he ate a tasteless energy bar. Tonight would be their last hot meal, and it was a miracle he'd tossed more extras in than he'd remembered. By tomorrow night they'd be getting hungry. Nothing serious; they weren't that far from Diablo and the Skagit River.

Maddy needed the calories more than he did. The effort she was making despite fever and pain was taking it out of her. In fact, not more than an hour later he glanced back and immediately knew she was about to hit the wall. She'd dropped back and her eyes looked glassy.

When they came to a small stream, one of the numerous tributaries carrying snowmelt down to join

Stetattle Creek and eventually the Skagit River, he decided the timing was perfect.

They crossed the stream on moss-covered rocks, more or less keeping dry, after which he led her upstream through the usual tangle until he found a mossy cove behind a cedar noticeably larger than any surrounding trees. A blackened scar on the trunk suggested it might have survived a forest fire that burned its compatriots.

Once again he spread the pad and sleeping bag before helping Maddy sit down. With a moan, she toppled onto her side, curling up.

Will laid a hand on her forehead. Speaking of burning. He needed to replace all her bandages to give himself a chance to search for obvious signs of infection. With nothing but soap and antibiotic cream, there wasn't much he could do, but that little would be better than nothing. For now, he'd let her rest.

MADDY COULDN'T SAY she felt better when she woke from her nap. Well...just lying down was a relief. She automatically turned her head until she saw Will partway around the tree sheltering them. Cradling a metal cup in his hands, he rested his back against the tree and sat with legs outstretched, crossed at the ankles. His brown hair was disheveled and the stubble on his jaw could now be described as a beard. His flannel shirt had tears, his jeans were dirty and his forearms and hands looked like he'd done battle with an annoyed bear.

Feeling a sting, she lifted her own arm. It was crisscrossed with angry scratches. More gingerly, she touched her cheek. Yep, face, too.

Will's head turned. "Nice nap?"

"I have no idea. It was more like lights out."

She loved the way his smiles both creased his cheeks and crinkled the skin beside his eyes.

"That was my impression," he agreed. "Lucky you weren't still standing up."

"I guess sleepwalking shows it's possible to do both things at the same time."

"Some soldiers will tell you they do it all the time."

She wanted to smile, but it was hard to move the muscles in her cheeks when her head ached the way it did. "I don't feel so good," she said after a minute.

"No," he said quietly, "you have a raging fever. Once you have a cup of coffee, I want to check all your wounds. We can clean up a little in this creek, too."

Without turning, Maddy couldn't see it, but she could hear a pleasant little ripple that was separate from the louder rush of Stetattle Creek.

"No dip in a deep pond?"

"Afraid not. Trust me, once you feel the temperature, you won't want to jump in."

The coffee energized her a little, and she popped some more pills.

Fifteen minutes later she discovered how right Will was. Still squeaking after yanking her hands out, she couldn't understand why the water was running and not frozen solid. Still, it was astonishingly clear and sparkled in the late-afternoon sun slanting through the tree branches.

She would have felt more self-conscious when she took her shirt off if Will's expression hadn't been so clinical. He examined her arm above and below the splint but decided not to take it off. He cleaned some grazes and gashes she'd almost forgotten about and then smeared ointment on them. After finding where the biggest lump had been on her head, he gave a grunt she took for satisfaction.

He removed her boots and socks himself, then helped her wriggle out of her jeans. That was when he saw something that made him mutter a sharp expletive.

Maddy twisted to try to see, too.

Even his gentle touch made her jump.

"It's infected, all right," he growled.

She couldn't get a good look at the spot she'd like to think was on her lower back but was probably actually her butt.

By the time he finished washing pus from what he said was an open cut, Maddy was gasping, her hands knotted into fists.

He must have said he was sorry ten times.

Eventually, he dug out clean jeans, shirt and underwear for her.

"I think you can do without these." He rolled up her pajama pants that had served as long underwear and stuffed them toward the bottom of the pack.

Then he left her on the mossy edge of the stream to wash.

"Call if you need me. I won't be far."

Ice-cold water or not, it felt good to wash everyplace she could reach. Although, wow, getting her hands on a razor jumped higher on her "I wish" list.

Still a few notches down from escaping a couple of merciless killers, of course.

As clean as she could make herself, she summoned Will, who buttoned the waist of her jeans and eased a T-shirt over her head and her splinted arm. He topped that with one of his sweatshirts, large enough to fit over the splint.

Squatting in front of her, rolling up the sleeves one at a time, Will once again demonstrated his extraordinary patience. His head bent, he concentrated on what he was doing, determined, Maddy knew, not to hurt her. How those big hands could be so deft and gentle both was a puzzle. She imagined him, suddenly, with a child. Watching him, she felt her heart cramp and her eyes sting. With the physical symptoms came the unsettling realization that she could love this man. Or maybe already did. Even the *idea* of saying goodbye to him was unimaginable.

If he didn't feel the same, she'd have no choice. She couldn't burden him with expectations he wouldn't want. Worse, he'd probably call what she felt *gratitude*.

Suddenly, she wanted to touch his beard. Find out whether it was wiry, prickly or soft. He probably wouldn't mind, but...

Sighing, she suddenly became aware that he'd rocked back on his heels and was looking straight at her, his expression quizzical. Blushing fiercely, she said, "Your turn. I'm, um, sorry the towel is so wet."

He only nodded. "Take it easy for a few minutes. I'll start dinner as soon as I'm done."

Maddy retreated to their campsite and sat on the sleeping bag with her back to him. She closed her eyes, listened for every tiny sound and resisted the temptation to peek.

WILL STUCK HIS head in the stream and used the soap to wash his hair. He did it as much to cool his over-heated body as because he cared whether his hair was grungy.

He'd give a lot to know what Maddy had been thinking to make her blush. Wondering was enough to tie his gut in a knot. It didn't seem to matter what he'd decided about the gulf between them. His body didn't want to hear it. And maybe he was wrong. Did any of those slick attorneys and businessmen in their custom-tailored suits *deserve* this gutsy woman?

Not in his book.

He did the best he could with the bar of soap and ice-cold water. Clean clothes felt good, although they'd be ripped, sweat-soaked and dirty an hour into their morning hike. Plus, it was his last set of clean clothes.

Will rubbed his hand reflectively over his jaw and neck. Damn, he did wish he could shave. He'd fre-quently let his beard go when on patrol, of course, but it invariably began to itch. He'd always scraped it off first thing.

Back at their campsite, Maddy sat unmoving. When she heard him, she burst out, "I wish I wasn't so useless."

"It's a miracle you aren't dead," he said brusquely. "Remember the part where you fell out of the sky?"

"Yes, but—" She pinched her lips together. "Never mind."

He crouched in front of her. "What's wrong, Maddy? What are you thinking?"

"I don't even know how to use a camp stove to heat water! And if I did, I probably couldn't anyway with only one hand."

"That's not it."

She averted her face. He used his knuckles beneath her chin to turn it back.

"I'm mad," she said suddenly. "They stole my life! I've had no say in anything for a year now. Do you know what that feels like?"

"Yeah," he said drily. "I was in the military."

"You chose it!"

Had he? Sure, he'd signed the papers, but given the freedom she'd taken for granted, he'd have chosen college, not becoming an army grunt.

But he said, "Once you testify, it'll all be over." In half the time of a two-year enlistment. He rose to his feet, but before he could go to his pack she grabbed the leg of his pants.

"Wait."

He did just that.

"I'm sorry. I despise whining. Plus, I sounded like a spoiled brat. I'm…not usually like that."

Will couldn't resist the plea in her hazel eyes. He crouched again to put himself closer to her level and said, "You're entitled to some whining. The past year has to have been frustrating and frightening both, and now you've had an epically bad few days. It's taken a lot of courage to go on the way you have. Does it really matter if you can't boil water?"

"No," she whispered. "You're right. Ignore me."

He shook his head. "That's not gonna happen, babe."

"Babe?"

He grinned. "Thought that'd get to you."

As he set up the small stove, he gave the fuel can a surreptitious shake. Not a lot left. Surely enough to boil water a few more times to make coffee.

Once he had it fired up, he asked for Maddy's menu preference.

"Pasta primavera," she said promptly.

While they ate, he asked her to tell him about the life she'd "lost"—although he didn't phrase it that way. He was curious, yes, but also needed to shore up his defenses.

She paused with her spoon in the packet. "Well… I had an apartment in West Seattle. Nice but not that fancy. I was lucky to find it given how expensive Seattle has gotten. At least I got to say goodbye to my parents, but I don't know if they are still paying the rent, or picked up my stuff and let the apartment go."

"Car?"

"Yes, because I needed it to see clients. I hardly ever drove it otherwise. Parking is hard to find, and you can get anywhere on the bus. There's a grocery store only half a mile from my place, and I like walking." She made a face. "I *used* to like walking."

Will smiled.

"I was seeing another attorney." She gazed into space for a minute then gave her head a shake. "I don't think it would have gone anywhere. I'm sure he's long since moved on."

"What if you get back and find he's been pining for you?"

"He won't be, but it doesn't matter. We had some fun, that's all. Anyway, I'm not the same person I was."

Will understood that. Her life had been flipped like a coin. Heads, everything was good. Tails, not so much. It was possible she'd slide back into her old life and gradually forget how it felt to be powerless, scared, on the run. She could build walls, or she could just be one of those people who deep down believed their lives were meant to be shiny. Yeah, bad things had happened, but they'd been temporary. A nuisance, that was all. Forgettable.

But he didn't believe that, not about Maddy.

He got her talking about her law firm and the kind of work she did. Since she'd been a defense attorney, it was probably no surprise after her experiences this past year that she admitted to wondering whether she should shift to become a public defender instead, or even a prosecutor.

"Although the woman, Laura Bessey, who I'd gone to see…" She hesitated. "The one who was murdered. She was dealing with both threats and weird stuff going wrong. She'd been fired from her job for reasons she claimed were pure fiction."

"You're assuming Brian Torkelson was behind all of it."

"Given that she'd decided she had to tell someone that he'd raped her, yes."

"Eat," he ordered her.

She looked startled, but lapsed into silence as she finished her meal. "That was surprisingly good," she commented.

"These freeze-dried meals taste a lot better than they look." His stomach still felt hollow, though, and he wondered if hers did, too. "Dessert?" he asked.

"Cherry pie à la mode?"

He laughed. "Almond Joy or Butterfinger."

"Maybe later." She looked around. "It's so pretty here. So green. The way the light is filtered through the trees makes me think of stained glass."

"This is magnificent country. First time I've ever climbed in the North Cascades, but it won't be the last."

Sadness crossed her face like a shadow. "Bill— the pilot—was pointing out these incredible peaks with names like Fury and, I don't know, Terror. I suppose people do climb them."

"Yeah, I'm hoping to find a partner to climb with and tackle one or two of them. Not sure I should go alone."

"No." She fell silent for longer than he liked, crinkles forming on her forehead. "I was just thinking I might like backpacking or climbing—although no thousand-foot drop-offs, thank you—only then it occurred to me that maybe this isn't the best time to be talking about the future."

"When better?" Will cleared some gruffness from his throat. "We're getting out of here, Maddy. My word on it."

"You shouldn't say that." She seemed to be looking deep inside him. "And I shouldn't believe you. But… I do." More softly, she added, "Or at least, I want to."

"Hold on to that," he said quietly. He took her hand in his and discovered it was easier to be optimistic when they had a physical connection.

SOMEBODY CRIED OUT. Maddy reeled back at the hideous sight, an awful stench in her nose and mouth.

"I'm sorry! I'm sorry!"

"Maddy!" Big hands shook her. "You're dreaming. It's not real."

Not real? In the darkness, she couldn't orient herself. Where was she? Who—

Will. Of course it was Will waking her from a nightmare. Somehow she'd pushed herself to a sitting position, and his arm supported her now.

She shuddered and turned her face into his chest. He kept soothing her until she mumbled, "I dreamed I was back there. At the crash site, where I found Bill and Scott. Only...only it was a day or two later and their bodies..."

"Maddy, they're dead. Unless a body is embalmed, that's what happens. Nature breaks down the flesh to return it to the earth."

The images from her nightmare were slipping away. "I know," she said after a minute. "I know." She swallowed. "Do you have nightmares?"

"I doubt there's a returning soldier who doesn't."

"So I have lots of company?"

"Yeah." Was that a smile in his voice? "You do. Including me. Now, lie down. You need your sleep."

"Okay." She tipped up her face impulsively to kiss his cheek. What she found was his mouth. Consternation mixed with excitement.

Before she could pull away, he'd lifted a hand to cup the back of her head.

"Maddy?"

That was all he said, but despite his hoarseness, she heard the question.

Chapter Eight

Her hand rose to his cheek, fingertips sampling his beard. Beard or no, Will felt her warmth. And her touch was answer enough, wasn't it?

He brushed her lips with his again, nibbled a little. She sucked in a breath and he took the chance to deepen the kiss. *Careful*, he told himself. He couldn't lay her down and expect her to take his weight. Even if she'd been uninjured and not half out of her mind with a fever…he couldn't take this that far. Not when she depended on him for her life. Not when he knew that what either of them felt right now might not be real.

But he savored this kiss, every quiver of her lips, the taste of her dinner and the mint of her toothpaste. Early Fourth of July fireworks. Will found himself squeezing her nape, so damn delicate. Deceptively delicate.

He lifted his head once so they could both breathe, then returned for more. Her response was eager as if she could keep kissing him forever. Will told himself he was good with that, except the bitter, too-proud kid he'd been started talking in his ear.

You roused her from a nightmare. Of course she's happy to kiss you! Great way to blot out the awful crap in her head.

The punch was a one-two.

Why wouldn't she kiss you? You've all but promised to die for her, if it comes to that.

The next time he needed oxygen, he kissed his way across her cheek, nuzzled her temple and laid her down. The inner voice was irritating but right. Anything like this had to wait.

"Sleep," he murmured. He didn't add, *Tomorrow is going to be a big day*, because that was a euphemism to end all euphemisms.

Tomorrow, he thought grimly, they'd likely come upon the surprise party. Given that they were massively out-gunned, their options weren't great.

When he stretched out beside Maddy, he noticed how stiffly she held herself. If she'd been able to turn her back to him, Will felt sure she'd have done it. He must have seemed abrupt, even to be rejecting her. Which, in a way, was what he'd done. For the best of motives. Somehow he doubted Maddy would see it that way.

Sleep wouldn't come easily. His empty belly alone wouldn't have kept him awake; he'd gone hungry plenty of times, both as a boy and as a soldier in the field. It was worries about tomorrow that held sleep at bay, along with second thoughts.

FERN FRONDS BRUSHING her face, Maddy sat hunched behind the roots of another fallen tree. This one might have fallen over the winter, or perhaps the year before. It hadn't taken long for the voracious vegetation to advance on the scar in the land. Nettles and devil's club seemed especially energetic.

Will had decided that today he'd scout ahead for each stretch then return for her. He'd done that twice already. She couldn't tell him how much she hated being left behind, or how afraid she was for him in these long interludes when she couldn't know what was happening to him. She clung to the memory of his kiss.

Infuriatingly, her arm and shoulder hurt worse when she sat still than they did when she moved. That probably wasn't really the case, but there wasn't much else to do but be aware of her body's complaints and listen for danger.

To top it all off, she itched fiercely beneath the splint on her arm, where of course she couldn't reach. Actually, she was afraid to move at all, partly because of the nettles. The back of her hand still stung from yesterday's carelessness. Mostly, though, she kept imagining watching eyes in the jungle around her. Every sound made her twitch. She listened for gunfire, knowing that even if Will managed to escape, it would take ages for him to make it back to her.

And if he didn't? What then?

He'd stuffed her pockets this morning with food:

dried fruit, a packet of peanuts and two candy bars. He didn't say anything, but then he hadn't had to. He wanted to be sure she had something to eat if she found herself on her own.

A heavy rustling among the alders and willows downstream brought her head up. Whoever was approaching didn't care about alerting anyone nearby to his presence. Were she and Will that noisy when they were on the move?

Please let this be Will.

Somehow, though, she knew it wasn't.

Maddy sat frozen, waiting, her eyes straining for the first sight. Her heart thudded. They hadn't yet found so much as a hint of a game trail this morning, but whoever—whatever—this was seemed to be coming straight toward her.

A crash among the whippy trunks and branches shook the leaves. Maddy tensed. She could run—

The something coming was huge…and black. A black bear. Not a grizzly; they were brown, weren't they?

Should she stay still and quiet and hope it never noticed her, or make lots of noise to try to scare it away?

More of the surrounding foliage shook. The bear wasn't twenty feet away when it stopped and the huge head swung toward Maddy. The nostrils quivered and they stared at each other.

Unable to sit still a second longer, Maddy jumped up, waved her arm and yelled, "Shoo!"

The bear lumbered straight toward her, using its

bulk to smash through the shrubs and small trees. Her head turned wildly. She couldn't run.

So she pressed among the tree roots, smelling the rank odor of bear even as it got so close she could see beady eyes and patchy fur.

At the last second it veered suddenly, continuing to crash away until Maddy heard a great splash. Bears probably didn't bother looking for fallen logs to cross a creek.

Her breath escaped in a big *whoosh* and her legs failed her. Butt in the dirt, she waited for her heartbeat to slow. Wilderness Girl she apparently wasn't.

Ten minutes later she heard someone/something else coming, but this one was a lot quieter than the bear had been. How he recognized where he'd left her, she didn't know, but by the time she made out Will, his gaze had already locked on to her.

"You okay?" he asked, sinking down beside her. His hair was full of twigs and leaves and debris and his arms and one cheek displayed new scratches. Sweat darkened his tan T-shirt and Maddy had no doubt the back of the shirt would be sweat-soaked, too, where he'd been carrying the pack. So far today he'd carried it with him during his reconnaissance, then stashed it somewhere for pickup once he returned with her.

Glad she'd had time to recover from the close encounter with the bear, she said, "Mostly. I had a scare when a bear passed only a few feet from me. I thought—"

In his usual calm way, he said, "Your typical

black bear is as afraid of you as you are of it. Cubs can change that, but the one you met might have been male."

Her attempt to read his expression didn't get her anywhere, so she finally asked, "Did you see anyone?"

He shook his head, weariness or maybe frustration finally showing. "Nope, but I don't believe they've given up."

"Do you want something to eat?" She extended the first thing her hand closed on, a box of raisins.

"No, thanks." He grabbed a tree root and pulled himself to his feet. "Let's keep moving."

She got up and fell in behind him, grateful when he parted the springy alder branches and held them until she was through, but also feeling guilty. Because she was so awkward and slow, Will was having to hike three times as far as she was. For at least the hundredth time, she silently acknowledged how lucky she was that he'd been here when she needed him.

"WE NEED TO cross the creek here," Will said. "I made it without getting wet, but the rocks are slippery."

Maddy nodded stoically. The bank ahead of them rose in an impassible, rocky, alder-infested cliff.

"Step where I do," Will told her, even knowing he didn't need to.

The constant mist above the fast-running creek provided a perfect environment for moss. The lower in elevation they progressed, the richer the moss. A pretty emerald green, it covered rocks, swallowed downed trees and enveloped anything that held still long enough. And, damn, it was slippery stuff underfoot, especially when wet.

He must be getting tired, because his mind jumped to how it had felt to kiss Maddy. Naturally, a foot skidded and he ended up shin deep in ice-cold water. Grimacing, Will pulled his foot out, shook it and set off again. Fortunately, with daintier feet, Maddy was having better luck staying dry.

Will had almost reached the far side when he heard a distant hum. Airplane? He looked up but didn't see anything in the blue arch of sky except clouds gathering over the Picket Range.

The sound grew, and he knew.

"Helicopter!" He reached back for Maddy's hand. "Hurry!"

He splashed through water for the last few steps and thought she did, too. Almost immediately, they entered the familiar snarl of willow and alder and devil's club, but he wasn't convinced the cover was sufficient to hide them from above. Neither of them wore bright colors, but even the greens and browns were subtly wrong.

They ran, or as close to running as they could do. The noise swelled, a swarm of angry bees. It could be a sightseeing helicopter or a search and rescue one heading to pick up an injured climber. Will didn't believe it, though.

A thick clump of lush sword ferns ahead looked

like their best bet. He and Maddy raced for it. At his direction, she wriggled among the ferns, lying prone, and Will followed. He pulled out the Glock and rolled onto his back, parting fronds until he had a view that was barely a slit.

Not twenty seconds later a black helicopter flying dangerously low came into sight. At almost the same moment, a deer in a panic struggled past. A good decoy, he thought. The helicopter kept moving, staying low.

As the racket receded, he murmured, "They're getting nervous. They're afraid they've lost us."

"They might have expected us to get down the mountain faster."

All he could see were her boots. He reached out and clasped her ankle because he needed to touch her. "They have to know you're injured." Even if their enemy hadn't gotten a good look at the two of them fleeing the hail of gunfire, people rarely walked away unscathed from a plane crash, especially one that had killed the pilot and the only other passenger.

Maddy didn't say anything.

Will's mind kept racing. How had these men accounted for him? Did they think they'd been misinformed and really there'd been a third passenger? Maybe even a second US marshal? If that were the case, they'd expect him to be armed.

Impatient with himself, he realized they already knew that. They would have found Marshal Rankin's body and the empty holster.

Will was torn between moving on and waiting to find out whether the helicopter would turn right around and retrace its path. Depended on how sure the two hunters on the ground were that he and Maddy had come this way. They might fear Will and she had climbed over the flank of McMillan Spire and down Terror and Goodell Creeks, as he and Maddy had discussed. If she hadn't been injured so badly, that might have been smart—except he reminded himself of the scarcity of cover at sub-alpine elevations.

He mulled over what the Forest Service personnel would think about the black, unmarked helicopter scaring the crap out of the wildlife, and what they could realistically do about it.

After venting a few words he should probably apologize for, Will said, "Let's keep moving. I left my pack in a good place to stop for a bite to eat."

"Okay."

When she struggled to roll over, he took her hand and pulled her to her feet. He didn't like that her face was bone-white except for those too-bright red spots on both cheeks. Fever. Even her hand was too hot.

Will liked even less knowing that despite all his training, he couldn't help her.

As they resumed their trek, broken branches gave evidence of the animals that had passed this way—and possibly of the men he still expected to encounter ahead. Will kept the pace slow for Maddy's sake and even his. He paused every few feet to listen, both for the helicopter returning and for the two gunmen. If

they'd been hunkered down here for two days, they
might have grown careless. Careless enough to talk,
to set a fire to dry out the socks and pant legs they'd
gotten wet when they slid on wet moss into the creek,
tumultuous with snowmelt.

The sound he did eventually hear was one he'd
expected. He'd left his pack close by where Torrent
Creek roared into Stetattle Creek.

His next task was to figure out whether there was
any easy way to get over Torrent, or whether they
needed to find a way to yet again cross to the other
side of Stetattle Creek. Shortly thereafter they'd
come on Jay Creek and several others joining their
waters to Stetattle, too. Each addition made their way
more perilous—and, damn, he wished he didn't feel
as if the two of them were obediently trotting like
cattle into a chute.

AN HOUR LATER the helicopter did pass over them
again. Will thought it hovered briefly a short distance downstream, but the density of the rain forest
growth meant he couldn't see it. Had it stopped to
drop off supplies? If so, had it flagged the trap he
and Maddy were meant to spring?

Fueled by determination and probably not much
else, Maddy kept going. They weren't more than a
hundred yards from Torrent Creek when he led her
deeper into the tangle to where he'd left his pack.

When he pulled out most of what he had left in the
way of food, Maddy shook her head and said dully,
"I'm not really hungry."

"Eat anyway." He handed her the water bottle. "Didn't I give you some raisins? Those should give you a boost."

A short one, about all sweets were good for.

For a moment she looked mulish, but after taking a long drink and returning the bottle to him, she produced the raisins and ate them slowly. Will confined himself to a small handful of almonds and a little bit of mixed dried fruit.

Then he pored over his contour map again. In theory, they'd reach this end of the Stetattle Creek trail in no more than an hour or two, depending on the difficulties they met during that distance. Unfortunately, from what he'd read in guidebooks, that didn't necessarily mean anything. In fact, it might not be possible to find any trace of trail there. It apparently wasn't maintained with any regularity. Only about the last mile, leading into the small town of Diablo, saw much traffic at all.

Still…if he were the gunmen, he'd set the ambush above Jay Creek, where the trail ended on the map. Hardy hikers must occasionally push on that far.

Will had no doubt these men would be willing to kill anybody who saw them, even a family. They must be aware that would make them hunted men, however. Most people would be missed almost right away.

Whereas if they could kill him and Maddy and carry their bodies even a few hundred yards from the creek, they might never be found. Will had registered for his climb, but would anyone really notice if he didn't reappear? Maybe after a while somebody would wonder about the abandoned Jeep, but that could take weeks. And Maddy had been on the plane that went down. If the pilot had filed a flight plan, there should already be a search in progress for the downed plane. If he hadn't, any search from the air would be happening well south of here. The route the small Cessna had taken deep into the North Cascades wasn't a logical one to deliver passengers to Everett.

When the plane was eventually found, rescue personnel would assume Maddy had lived but was direly injured and had wandered away. She could be anywhere. By that time—a minimum of a week after the plane went down?—the chances of her still being alive would be considered minimal.

It was just too bad that Judge Brian Torkelson's minions knew she wasn't dead.

Will especially disliked leaving Maddy this time, but he wanted to complete another leg of their hike out before stopping for the night. He shouldered his pack again and looked down at her. He'd swear she'd lost more weight than should be possible in a matter of only days.

She gazed up at him. "Be careful, Will."

She'd been sitting close enough to see the map as he studied it and would have reached the same conclusion he had: they were close to the spot where they were meant to die.

"I will." He hesitated. "If you want to lie down and rest, I can put a few branches on top of you."

"There's not much I could do if I were awake anyway, is there?"

No. He'd actually considered leaving the Glock with her, but remembered her holding it in shaking hands when he first came on her. All she had to do was panic and shoot a bear or deer and she'd give away their location.

He wasn't convinced she could pull the trigger to kill someone anyway.

If he, on the other hand, had a chance to take out one of the men, he wouldn't hesitate.

So he used his pocketknife to cut a few willow and alder branches, laid them gently atop her and said, "Sleep tight."

Walking away, Will wished she'd laughed. Her retreat into silence told him that either the pain was wearing her down, or the infection was gaining ground.

On his own, with no enemy between him and civilization, he could have pushed on and been in Diablo before dark. As it was, even if they could get past the gunmen, nothing he'd read about the trail made him think it was navigable by flashlight. Which meant another night.

When he glanced back, he discovered Maddy was already lost from his sight.

Will moved as carefully as he could, stopping every few strides to listen, to look. If he was right, the two men weren't mountain climbers or even necessarily hikers. They were probably ex-military, which gave them some skill, but not any level of

comfort with a landscape so different from any in
Iraq or Afghanistan.

Will could say the same about himself, except
he and several high school friends had done some
climbing up here and in the Olympic Mountains.
They'd climbed Mount Shasta first, of course, the
volcano in their own neighborhood. Then they'd done
Mount Rainier. The summer after his high school
graduation and right before he enlisted, they came
up to climb Glacier Peak, the most inaccessible of
the northwest volcanoes and possibly the toughest
climb, too. They'd been lucky to hook up with a
couple of men who actually knew what they were
doing. Standing on the summit of Glacier had been
one of the more exhilarating moments of Will's life.

Maybe that was what he was doing up here in the
North Cascades: trying to recapture remembered
happiness. Except that this time he hadn't climbed
with friends or even strangers. He'd have said he
was best off on his own…until he'd found Maddy.

He watched for a chance of crossing Stetattle
along here, but could see that wasn't an option. The
land on the far side climbed too steeply from the
creek. That meant they instead had to cross Torrent
Creek…which would be an ideal place to set a trap.

When he knew he was getting close, Will left his
pack behind and bent low as he crept forward, trying not to so much as shake the leaves. Long training and experience allowed him to become a ghost.
He was hunting. His sharpened senses threw him

back until momentarily the where and when blurred in his mind.

But the nonstop roar of the waterfalls that made up Torrent Creek as it plunged from near the summit of Elephant Butte pulled him back to the present. When the white water tumbling over rocks came into sight, he lifted his binoculars and began his search.

A tiny movement, a glint of something metallic, gave them away. He zeroed in on them, wishing he was looking through a rifle scope rather than binoculars. No such luck, and they were well out of range of a handgun.

Wearing the green camouflage that blended eerily well with the lush surroundings, they had set up above a fallen tree that made a convenient bridge across Torrent Creek. From where Will crouched, it appeared to be the *only* way to cross.

One of the two men lay on his belly with his AR-47 on a bipod. Behind him and screened by a few twisted alders and what might be a cedar, the second man sat with his back to the trunk of a large fir. His hands moved… He was eating. Will couldn't quite tell what. His own stomach cramped but his awakened rage made it easy to ignore his physical needs.

These men were prepared to kill a courageous, smart, sweet woman who'd done nothing wrong. No principles involved, no issues of national security, nothing personal at all, just a paycheck. That, or they actively enjoyed hunting their fellow humans. With no conscience, no empathy, the type sometimes made good soldiers—unless an occasion came when they had to depend on their own judgment.

Will had never trained to be a sniper, never wanted to be one, but he'd just changed his mind. Too late.

Now came the hard part: finding a way around the ambush…or a way to take out the men.

Chapter Nine

Maddy started awake, gasping from some horror already dissolving as most dreams did. Opening her eyes to find branches in her face added a jolt, too, until she remembered where she was and why. Then…then she felt as if they were a cozy comforter Will had tucked around her.

She hurt so much. Maddy hadn't said anything to Will, because she heard the rattle of the remaining pills in the bottle each time he doled out painkillers. They were almost gone. He hadn't been taking any that she could see, and she suspected he hurt, too.

If only she had a watch or her phone so she'd know what time it was and how long Will had been gone.

Instead of sitting up, she stayed where she was, curled on her side. She could see where Will would emerge when he returned.

Although she drifted some, she didn't think it was more than another ten minutes or so when he did appear. To her surprise, he still carried the pack.

"You didn't leave it?"

"I want to stay here for the night." His expression was very closed, but anger leaked through.

Pushing branches away, Maddy squirmed until she could push herself up to a sitting position. "What is it? Did you see them?"

In the act of unzipping his pack, he flicked a glance at her. "I did. They're set up just across Torrent Creek where it enters Stetattle. They found the obvious place to cross and assume we're dumb enough to use it."

"What are we going to do?"

The gray of his eyes had chilled, leaving her in no doubt that the soldier had taken the forefront. "I scouted farther up and found another way across. It's...not easy to get to, and scary as hell. The log isn't more than about ten inches in diameter. We'll have to shimmy across on our butts, and, damn, I wish I'd brought a rope."

"Okay," she said, refusing to surrender to fear. Or maybe she was just too tired, hurt too much, to be bothered by the possibility of an awful outcome.

Will studied her broodingly. "We'll see how you feel tomorrow. There is an alternative."

His grim tone awakened apprehension in her. "What is it? Are you...you won't leave me and go for help, will you?"

"No, although that might be smart." He frowned. "Which reminds me..." Suddenly, he began digging in his pack. He came up with a smartphone. "I wonder...hey, look at that. About time the damn phone isn't just deadweight. I might be able to make a call."

"You can't!" she exclaimed in alarm.

"Wouldn't it be better to trust some search and rescue people than die?" he asked harshly.

"You think Torkelson doesn't have someone watching for anyone carried out of the park?" she scoffed. "It's not that hard to get to someone in the hospital, and that's assuming they're not waiting at the trailhead to gun me and everyone else down."

He stared at her without blinking for at least a minute. Then, muttering something she was glad not to have heard, he dropped the phone, scrubbed both hands over his face and let his shoulders sag. "I do know that. But you have a fever, we aren't eating enough and every step must hurt like hell. Now I'm telling you we have to climb an extra thousand feet or so, scoot on our butts over a raging torrent, then whack our way across a steep downslope to get behind these—" He swallowed whatever he'd meant to call them. "Oh, and assuming we succeed, we then have several *more* miles of bushwhacking and river crossings to go."

"I can—"

As if she hadn't opened her mouth, he shook his head and said, "Maybe plan B makes the most sense."

Bothered by his expression, the way the muscles in his cheeks and jaw had tightened, Maddy asked, "And what's that?"

"I cross without you, circle behind the bastards and kill them."

"Execute them."

His eyes no longer gave away any emotion at all. "If all goes well."

Feeling semi-hysterical, she said, "You mean, if they don't see you in time to kill *you*."

"That would be the downside." He didn't shrug, but he might as well have. *Hey, no biggie*, he was saying.

Spitting mad, she snapped, "You think I don't *care* if you die?"

"It's been my worry all along that if anything happens to me, you're screwed."

"I should just worry about myself? Like you don't *matter*?"

Now he looked faintly wary. "I didn't say that."

"You did! I'd rather die myself than have you do something that...that stupid!"

He blinked a couple of times. "We're at war, Maddy."

"Maybe we are, but we both have to make it out of here. Besides..."

His eyebrows climbed. "Besides?"

"To kill two men you don't know from behind seems wrong. I mean, this is America. You fought for the rights we believe in, for due process."

His reaction was somewhere between pity and a sneer. "In battle you don't give someone a chance to say, 'Oh, sorry, didn't really mean to shoot you.' Not when their damn gun is pointing at your head. Those two SOBs already tried to strafe us. Now they're set up in a blind waiting for us to walk into range. When I saw them, one lay in classic sniper position with his rifle positioned on a bipod. What do you think, I should shout across the river, 'We'll give you a chance to do the right thing and pack up and leave'?"

When he put it that way, Maddy felt foolish. Of course he was right. She realized that what bothered her wasn't so much the idea of bloodshed as it was what summarily killing those two men would do to Will. He hadn't said so, but he'd come back from war injured badly enough to need many months of rehab. He could well be dealing with some PTSD. He maintained internal walls that had to be hiding something. And now, thanks to her, he was thrown back into battle.

She didn't want to be the reason he had to kill.

"I've made it this far," she said, chin up. "I feel lousy, but I'm not on the verge of collapse. I can climb, and crossing the creek on a skinny log will probably be harder for you than me—"

"Except that you'll be doing it one-handed."

Holding his gaze, Maddy made sure he saw her determination. "If I have to, I'll take my arm out of the sling. It won't kill me."

"Not a good idea."

Eyes locked, they held a stare, neither wanting to back down. In the end, Will relented.

"We'll try it your way."

"Thank you."

He grunted and said, "Let me fire up the stove to heat water for coffee. I'll make sure we have enough for a morning cup, too. I want us to make an early start."

Maddy nodded, even as she couldn't help thinking sleep wouldn't come easily tonight given the worries that were bound to get in the way.

DEEP SHADOWS REACHED them long before sunset. Will had earlier laid out the pad and sleeping bag. Maddy and he sat on it, her cross-legged, him with long legs outstretched. Clouds blocked the moon and had him grumbling about the possibility of rain. Naturally, he had a tarp folded in his pack, which he took out in case of need.

Dinner consisted of a few nuts and a candy bar for her, an energy bar for him. Maddy had a suspicion he hadn't fairly divided the nuts, and called him out on it.

Those broad shoulders lifted. "I've gone without food plenty of times in my life. You're more vulnerable right now. I'll stay strong for a few more days."

She wanted to object, but couldn't. Her stomach was already taking sharp exception to the news that a nice stir-fry or pizza or a juicy hamburger weren't forthcoming.

"You know," he remarked, "if I took those two worthless bastards out, we could raid their packs for food."

The thread of humor in his voice sparked hers.

"Okay, that's tempting…but no."

"Yeah, thought you'd say that."

The night wasn't entirely silent. She could hear the creek, rustles all around them. Bats darted into sight and out of it as fast. Mosquitoes whined and she or Will would slap irritably at them. A series of hoots almost had to be from an owl. Once a darker bulk waddled by not ten feet from them.

"Porcupine," Will murmured.

She held her breath until it was gone. "Thank goodness we haven't met up with one."

"They're nocturnal."

"Oh." Maddy was beginning to realize how ignorant she was about everything from the geology of these mountains to the birds and flowers, mammals and fish that made their home here. Today she'd noticed mushrooms beneath trees and she'd caught sight of a lizard. Except for the flies and—whack!— the mosquitoes, she didn't even recognize the insects.

Once it was safely dark, she said, "You don't have to answer, but… I was wondering if you have PTSD."

Will didn't move for a long time. She couldn't even hear him breathe. At last he said slowly, "Sure, to some degree. Most of us who've seen much combat probably do. I'm holding it together, if that's what you're asking."

"No." Maddy reached out blindly to lay a hand on his arm. "I wondered, that's all."

He covered her hand with his. "I've needed more solitude and quiet than usual. I don't love cities. That's…something I'll have to get over if I go—"

Despite the way his hand tightened on hers, she asked, "Go where?"

"Oh, maybe back to school. I haven't decided."

His tone held a warning. He didn't want to tell her his plans. That stung, since he knew everything

about her. She had to remind herself that he had no
obligation to balance the scales. He'd jumped in to
save her life, not to become her best friend or more.

And that, Maddy knew suddenly, was why his retreat hurt. She was falling in love with this man, and
obviously the feeling wasn't reciprocated.

She started the laborious process of getting up. "I
think I'll brush my teeth now."

Without argument, he reached for the pack where
he kept their toiletries.

HOLDING MADDY IN his arms, Will looked up at the
canopy of trees and the complete darkness beyond
that told him clouds still blocked the moon. He
wasn't at all sleepy.

Part of his tension had to do with Maddy, who
he suspected was pretending she was asleep. The
few last words they'd exchanged had been practical.
Once they'd arranged themselves on the pad, covered
by the open sleeping bag, she'd said, "Good night,"
which he'd echoed. Nothing since.

He knew what she felt like asleep, and this wasn't
it. He also knew he was responsible for her withdrawal. Kissing her had scared him. Even thinking about telling her his plans—better labeled as
hopes—stirred up his insecurities.

If he couldn't get over his inferiority complex,
he'd have to walk away from her once he knew she
was safe to go on with her life. Was that what he
wanted?

No. And yes. He couldn't stand hearing con-

descension or the wrong brand of kindness from
Maddy, of all people.

"You okay?" he asked softly.

"Mmm."

Will smiled. Stubborn woman was giving him the
silent treatment, which he deserved.

"I'm sorry," he said a minute later.

Sounding sincere but frosty, she said, "You have
nothing to be sorry for."

He was still smiling, he realized. Maybe that was
what pushed him over. "I'm hoping to go to medical
school. I've been studying for the MCAT."

"Will!" She lifted her head, although he knew
she couldn't really see him. "That's wonderful. The
years as a medic have to be a big plus."

"I hope so," he said a little stiffly. The training
had been far more extensive than even a stateside
paramedic received. In the midst of battle, military
medics had to act without concern for their personal
safety. With even a field hospital often hours away,
they sometimes even had to perform rough and ready
surgery.

"Are you already set on a branch of medicine?"

He hesitated. "No. Maybe trauma, but—" He'd
seen too many broken, bleeding bodies already "—I
like the idea of family medicine. Being the first line
of defense."

"I like that." She laid her head on his shoulder again
and wriggled a little as if burrowing in closer. "You'll
be an amazing doctor. I can give you a testimonial."

Will chuckled. "I'll keep that in mind. Now, go to sleep."

Good advice.

Actually, once he knew she slept, he allowed himself to drop off, too.

Barely past dawn, they each had a cup of coffee—a little weak, since he was running out—and ate the last of their food. He gave her the last painkillers, too. If they could get around the trap, he could carry her if he had to.

Not *if*, Will told himself. When. A positive attitude worked.

Even so, today was their fifth day.

Half an hour of bushwhacking brought them within twenty yards or so of where he'd crouched yesterday and spotted the gunmen. During the hike he'd made the decision to leave his pack behind. He'd take the few essentials in it—his car keys, phone, wallet, binoculars and the Glock as well as the ice ax, while making absolutely certain there wasn't anything left that could be used to identify him. He asked Maddy if she was especially attached to anything. She pondered and shook her head. If they were stuck out here for another night, he might be sorry, but he needed to be able to help her and to move quietly and swiftly.

Leaving her, he crept forward again. The sky was still pearly, but damned if the men weren't in position and appearing alert. He studied them carefully, in part to be sure they were the same two he'd seen. He'd worried all along that there could be more than two. If he was right in thinking the helicopter had stopped to hover near them yesterday, it could have been dropping off more troops.

Personally, if he'd been setting up this op, he'd have left one man in position where they were while having the other work his way up that side of Torrent Creek in case his quarry did exactly what he and Maddy intended to do. His gut said these two were overconfident, smugly certain the woman injured in the plane crash and whatever man accompanied her wouldn't have the backcountry expertise or the stamina to overcome the challenges.

He went back for Maddy, and they began the tortuous trek up the steep slope above the creek plummeting down from the mountain above.

MADDY DIDN'T KNOW how she could go on. She'd quit caring if she lived or died. She thought she'd have collapsed long since if she hadn't assured Will she could do this. Pride. What stupid motivation.

If it works…

She reached for a sturdy alder branch, drew a deep breath and heaved herself up. Her chest and shoulder exploded with pain. In the distant reaches of her head, she knew that every time she used her arm to pull herself upwards, she did bad things to the broken ends of her collarbone, even if the damage was on the other side of her chest. In between, the agony would subside to a dull ache, but this…

I can't do it. I shouldn't have said I could.

He'd given her the last ibuprofen this morning, only two pills.

Will paused and turned back, the worry on his face giving her the strength to reach for his hand and let him hoist her the next few feet.

Same result: pain that felt like a knife thrust into her shoulder and twisted. Her vision dimmed, but she focused on his eyes, as dark as charcoal right now.

He knows.

"We're almost there," he said in a low voice. "You're doing great. Five more minutes."

Five more minutes. She couldn't do this.

Yes, she could. *Five more minutes.* She took his hand again.

A branch whipped across her face. Maddy knew without touching her cheek that she was bleeding. At least it hadn't struck her across the eyes.

Five more minutes.

"Almost there."

If she could just *rest.*

"We're here, sweetheart. We can take a break."

His tenderness made her eyes sting. With an arm around her waist, he lowered her to sit on a rock. It was a minute before the pain abated enough for her to take a look at the log lying across the head of a viciously foaming cataract. If she fell…well, the first rocks she'd hit were only about ten feet below, but then she'd be bounced—or swept by the white water—down another ten feet, and another.

Scary. Wasn't that the word Will had used?

Normally, she'd be able to stroll right across it, if only it wasn't soaking wet.

Close behind her, Will was scanning the other bank through the binoculars. Not looking entirely happy, he slung the strap across his body again.

"Looks like we're alone up here."

She nodded, because it seemed like the thing to do.

He growled suddenly. "I'd give anything to be able to rope you up while you cross."

"What about you? You're so much bigger. What if—" Maddy couldn't finish.

His mouth twisted into a smile. "I'll be okay. Promise."

She tried to smile, too, when she wanted to grab hold and never let go. She didn't know why he hadn't kissed her again, but...

His head bent to hers. "How about a kiss for luck?"

Unhesitating, thankful, Maddy lifted her face to his. The kiss was achingly gentle, heart-wrenchingly sweet. She forgot the pain, forgot what lay ahead of them, lost herself in a kiss nothing like any she'd experienced. When it ended, she barely held back from saying, *I love you*. This might be the right moment...but it could as well be the worst of moments.

INCHING ALONG THE log that lay over Torrent Creek was the most hair-raising thing Will had done in a long while, and that included some journeys through dark, narrowing sandstone caves, crouching behind

Brace for Impact

a tree or rock formation half his size as a troop of Taliban wound its way past only feet away from him.

This was damned uncomfortable for a man, besides. He'd never had a problem with heights, but he was going to make an exception for this. The idea of slipping off, not being able to catch himself, hearing Maddy's cry...

He forced himself to concentrate on what he was doing.

He'd like to feel relief when he reached the other side, but his tension only ratcheted up. Watching Maddy scooting over the skinny log above the torrent, only able to use one hand to propel herself, was going to be one of the hardest things he'd ever done.

He blew out air, rolled his shoulders, finally taking a minute to search the overgrown creek valley through the binoculars. Nothing stood out.

Didn't mean he could relax.

He had to hold on to his self-control with both hands when he called over the roar of falling water, "Your turn."

It killed him just watching how long it took her to rise to her feet. She stumbled once reaching the bank. Will closed his eyes. He would do *anything*... but couldn't help at all.

She straddled the log the way he had, scooted forward two or three times then stopped and worked the sling past her elbow, slipping her arm out of it. He kept his mouth clamped shut. Whether she could stand the pain if she had to clamp hold with both arms, he didn't know, but having the arm free if she started to slide was smart.

Maddy winced as she cautiously straightened her injured arm before pulling it back against her body. Still, with just the one hand on the log, she scooted forward again, and again.

Will stood on the bank, his hands flexing into fists, loosening, knotting. He'd have paced, except he couldn't take his eyes off her.

Spray shimmered on her hair. She didn't look at him at all. Instead, she stared at the log just in front of her with burning intensity.

"Come on, come on," he chanted under his breath. "You can do it. Keep going. That's it."

She passed halfway. A moment later she wobbled, reached out with her injured arm and steadied herself. He thought she cried out, but he couldn't hear her. She immediately bent forward, cradling her arm.

Shuddering, Will felt rooted where he was. His knuckles ached and his fingernails bit into his palms.

"Keep going. Please. Keep going."

Maddy never looked up. Just slowly straightened, stared fixedly ahead of herself and resumed inching forward.

The moment she cleared the bank, he snatched her up into his arms.

Chapter Ten

Will thought they were at an elevation of between fifteen hundred and two thousand feet. Maddy wondered why he cared. They were slipping and slithering along a side hill that wasn't as steep as where they'd been when this all began, but was difficult going anyway. Especially since she so often had to grab a branch for support, wrenching her torso and collarbone. Even so, it was initially a relief compared to their trek straight uphill.

Fifteen minutes along, her thigh muscles and ankles began to protest. The positive was that they were moving slowly. Will obviously intended to be ultra-careful.

They had barely exchanged a word since they left Torrent Creek behind. Maddy knew they were passing right above the murderous pair still lying in wait, maybe as little as five hundred feet separating them. If one of them decided to scout around...

She clenched her teeth to keep any gasps from escaping.

They came to yet another creek carrying snowmelt from above. It wasn't as wide or powerful as Torrent Creek, but Will left her to hunt for a safe way to cross. They ended up descending to a place where they could scramble over on mossy rocks. One of her feet got soaked, as did one of his. She dismissed the squishy feeling as a minor discomfort.

Sometime in the next hour, Will began angling them downward. Instead of the miserable creek-bed jungle they'd previously beaten their way through, this was a magnificent forest. Maddy recognized big-leaf maples mixed into evergreens, including a few massive trunks of ancient trees. It was so green everywhere she looked. Moss grew everywhere, and lacy swags of pale green and gray draped from branches. Lichen, Will told her.

They were so close. She'd looked at the map enough to know they would meet up with the Stetattle Creek trail anytime. And yes, Will had read that the upper half or more wasn't maintained, but at least there'd *been* a trail there once upon a time. That had to be better than the completely untamed wilderness they'd been crossing, didn't it?

They ended up finding a remnant of the trail by accident. This time it was Will who lost his footing. Swearing, he skidded down a sharp drop-off and, from her perspective, thudded to a sudden stop.

"Hot damn," he said. "It's flat here, Maddy. See if you can get down on your feet instead of your ass like I did."

There were purple berries on one of the shrubs.

She reached out without thinking, made herself
ask, "Will? There are berries here. Are they edible?"

"Purple?"

"Yes."

"Huckleberries. Good eating."

Maddy picked and stuffed several handfuls into
her mouth before cautiously picking her way down
to him, where she found him doing the same.

"We'd probably better not have any more." The
hand that reached for her was stained purple. So was
hers, for that matter. "Don't know how much our
stomachs can handle. Besides…"

Besides, they were so close to escaping.

Without a word, she set off behind him.

WITHIN MINUTES THE trail vanished, having clearly
fallen victim to a washout. Will had to lead Maddy
up a sharp climb before angling back down again.
Another creek emerged from a sharp cut in the slope.
This time he and Maddy simply scrambled through
it, past caring about wet boots.

He started paying attention to the sun. More hours
had passed than he'd realized, which lessened their
chances of meeting a party of hikers coming up from
Diablo. Will really didn't want anyone else to set
eyes on Maddy.

As they kept moving, he became increasingly
wary, stopping her at regular intervals to listen and
look, both ahead and behind. Anyone pursuing them
would expect them to pop out in the tiny hamlet of
Diablo. Given how major the operation was that had

been set in motion to find her, Will expected that someone would be hanging out between here and the parking lot, waiting for them.

Twice more they had to detour around stretches where the trail was missing, a tree had fallen or a rockfall presented an impassable obstacle. Eventually, the trail began a series of switchbacks taking the steep drop back to the creek. Maddy plodded along, looking at where she was placing her feet. She never lifted her head, even when a doe splashed through yet another tributary right in front of them.

But damn, she was still walking. The strange swelling in his chest, Will finally identified as pride. She'd insisted she could do this, and she had.

Almost.

Just as he started to feel complacent, he heard a voice, followed by a younger, excited one. He turned his head. There.

He grabbed Maddy's arm and steered her up and over a giant fallen tree, rotting and moss-covered. Beyond was a lush cluster of ferns and the hated devil's club. Will coaxed her into lying down but hadn't gotten that far himself when a man and two boys appeared on the trail.

Will smiled and nodded.

"Whatcha doing?" the younger boy asked.

"Having a snack," he said, picking a few berries to demonstrate.

"Oh. Dad, can we…?"

"They're thicker just a little ways up the trail,"

Will put in. He held up his hand in illustration. "I just decided to grab a last few."

The man, balding and wearing running shoes, said, "Come on, boys."

"There's a landslide and some washouts ahead," Will warned. "You can get around them, but it's a scramble."

With a thanks, the small group moved on. The minute they were out of sight, Will helped Maddy back to her feet, over the log and down the trail.

Even over the gurgle of the creek, he heard the sound of a car engine.

He kept her behind him along the last, short stretch until buildings came into sight. The whole way, his hand hovered over the butt of the Glock. He had to find a place to hide her while he went to get his Jeep.

He spotted what appeared to be a garage. He could drive right up to it.

He steered her around behind it. "Okay, honey, I want you to wait here for me. I'll get the car and come back for you."

Comprehension was slow in coming, but finally she nodded.

To cheer her up, he said, "There's nowhere to eat in Diablo, not even a store, so it's just as well we don't want to hang around anyway. The first real town we come to that has a drive-through burger joint, we're stopping." He didn't mention that it would be some miles. On the map, Newhalem looked like a town but was really just housing for National Park Service and Seattle City Light employees. He was pretty sure there was nothing like a restaurant there.

Maddy's lips were cracked. Damn it, had she been biting them? But those lips also curved. In a croaky voice, she said, "I want a root beer float."

Will grinned at her. "You can have anything your heart desires."

Her eyes more alert, she said, "I'm okay. Go."

Hating to leave her, Will did anyway, strolling as if he wasn't in any hurry at all. A man sitting in an SUV seemed to be watching him…or happened to be idly gazing in his direction. Hard to be sure, but what could he be waiting for? Will nodded in a friendly way then let his own gaze wander.

The hair on his neck prickled when he saw a beefy guy wearing camo cargo pants, a dark green T-shirt and boots striding across the narrow bridge that led into town. The guy looked him over but seemed to dismiss him when Will veered into the parking area and unlocked his Jeep.

Will hated situations like this. He'd lost track of days, but he knew there were too many people around. With this having been the Fourth of July weekend, the campground and trail around the lake were undoubtedly still packed. Plenty of people would have taken a week off. This time of year, climbers and hikers came and went constantly. He hoped he didn't stand out.

If a watcher had noted the Jeep sitting here for over a week and then saw a man who wasn't carrying a pack strolling out of the forest and hopping in, that might catch his attention. Especially when that man didn't head over the bridge to the highway, but instead drove back to the trailhead.

Couldn't be helped—but he'd keep the Glock close at hand.

MADDY HEARD VOICES and car engines, but didn't see anyone as she waited. Still, she felt exposed. She let herself lean on the clapboard wall, but not sit. She knew how hard it would be to get up again.

The growling sound of an engine coming closer made her feel like a rabbit that unexpectedly found itself in the open when a coyote prowled toward it. *Please be Will*, she thought.

It was. He startled her by coming an unexpected way around the building.

He said only, "Let's get out of here," and hustled her into the backseat. "Lie down. I'm going to throw some stuff on top of you."

She crawled in, and seconds later was buried by what she thought was a parka and a blue tarp. A thump was the descent of a boot right beside her head. She couldn't tell where the other boot went.

"Keep down until I tell you otherwise," he said tersely.

The door slammed. The driver-side door opened and closed, and they were moving. They stopped briefly—

"Bridge is narrow," he said, voice low. "I'm letting a camper cross."

Rattling as they passed across the bridge, then the smoother whir of tires on a highway.

"Stay there for a few minutes," Will said, his tone normal. "I want to be sure no one follows us."

A part of her wanted to sit up and *see*, but the motion of the vehicle and the hum of the engine also made her sleepy. She blinked awake when Will said sharply, "Maddy! Are you okay?"

"I…" She worked her mouth. "Yes."

"I think you can sit up if you want."

"I'm kind of comfortable," she admitted.

He laughed. "Okay. Tell you the truth, I'm afraid we won't find a drive-through until we get to Rockport, and that's, I don't know, fifteen, twenty miles."

"Okay," she mumbled, and went back to sleep.

She woke up again when they reached the town of Rockport, but at his suggestion stayed where she was while he went through the drive-through and asked for three cheeseburgers, three orders of French fries, a Coke and a root beer float. Only after he paid, collected the food and pulled out did she untangle herself from the debris on the backseat and sit up.

She'd barely gotten a quick view of lake, trees, mountains, when Will snapped, "Get back down. *Now.*"

Without hesitation, she followed his order, yanking stuff over her with her good hand. "What is it?" she whispered.

"I recognize the SUV behind us." He swore. "I didn't see it when I pulled into the eatery, but if he was hanging back…" Pause. "I think I'll eat and dawdle along, see if he won't give up and pass us."

Her stomach growled and her mouth watered at the smell of burger and fries and the sounds of Will eating, but she lay still, her pulse racing. To get so far and then be caught. They couldn't be so unlucky, could they?

The minutes ticked by. Then, "Yep, there he goes," Will said, but tension remained in his voice. "He took a good look at me as he went by."

"He can't know it's you."

"No, there's no way they got much of a look at me the one time we know they saw us. I'm not wearing the same shirt, and I have plain brown hair. I just hope he's satisfied that I'm alone."

"Can I sit on the floor back here and eat?" She sounded pitiful and didn't care. "I'll duck further down if you tell me to."

"Yeah."

Given the length of his legs, it wasn't surprising that his seat was pushed back so far. Maddy squeezed herself onto the floor on the passenger seat.

Will handed back a bag, then the tall cup with her float.

The salty French fries she crammed into her mouth might taste better than anything she'd ever eaten.

WILL MANAGED TO down his double meal with no trouble even as he kept a sharp eye out during the remainder of the drive, especially when he reached the turn-off from Highway 20 in Concrete. He was renting a log cabin in what seemed like the middle of nowhere, just the way he'd wanted it. Now he didn't love the fact that his cabin was at the end of the road, with no neighbors near enough to hear or see any visitors. Fortunately, he hadn't yet changed the address for his driver's license or car registration from the barracks at Fort Lewis, the army base by Tacoma. He'd be surprised if somebody hadn't noted his license plate number, probably along with others. He couldn't think of any way they'd track him by it, though. Even the army didn't know where he was.

Relaxing, he said, "You can get up if you want. We're almost home."

His home, he reminded himself, not hers. A successful Seattle attorney wouldn't want to live in the back of beyond, even if the commute was possible. Which it wasn't. No, he was giving her temporary refuge, that was all. He couldn't afford to get any ideas.

He heard her struggling to get back up onto the seat. There was a silence as she looked around.

"This doesn't look any different than it did up there." Her surprise was obvious.

"No, my cabin is just outside the Mount Baker National Forest. I don't know if this is technically rain forest, but it feels like it. The things draping from tree limbs are a form of lichen like Old Man's Beard. Takes a really wet climate for them to survive. Looks like someone toilet-papered the trees and no one bothered to clean up, but they grow from the branches. Sort of a moocher, I guess."

"Like me," she said, so softly he suspected he wasn't meant to hear.

The comment gave him a pang. Maddy was no user.

"I don't know about you," he said, "but I'm looking forward to a shower. Wanna race?"

Caught in the rearview mirror, her smile was weak but present.

She'd stiffened up, accepting his help to climb out of the Jeep. Her head turned as she took in the open forest, the green light filtering through high fir, cedar and hemlock boughs, the peace. The only sound was the ripple of a small creek that the back deck looked down on.

"It's beautiful." Her voice was hushed in keeping with the atmosphere.

"I think so," he agreed.

He unlocked the front door and led Maddy in. The space was open, the only walls enclosing the bathroom. Steps almost steep enough to be a ladder led up to a loft, where he slept. A cast-iron stove sat in front of the river rock chimney. Hewn of fir, the kitchen cabinets fit with the glossy log walls and small-paned windows. Will was going to hate to leave this place when the time came.

He nudged Maddy straight into the bathroom and sat her down on the closed toilet seat. There he helped her strip to bra and panties, trying desperately to look at her from the perspective of a medic, not a man who wanted her.

It didn't prove to be as difficult as he might have thought, not once he got a good look at how battered she was. She'd acquired plenty of new bruises, as he probably had, too. The lump on her collarbone had enlarged and felt hot to the touch. The gash he already knew was infected was violently red around the edges and filled with pus. The only good news he could find was that the bumps on her head were gone.

His close inspection, he noticed, had brought pink color to her grimy cheeks. Pretending he didn't realize she felt self-conscious, he said, "Okay, pain meds, then shower. If you need help washing your hair, give me a yell. While you're in there, I'll find you something clean to wear and a real, honest-to-goodness sling. I'll call my doctor friend for an antibiotic prescription, too." He sat back on his heels. "You up to this?"

She might look like hell, but she managed a smile. "A shower? Are you kidding?"

He laughed, shook out a couple of the strongest pain pills he had and gave them to her with a glass of water. Surreptitiously, he pocketed a couple of them himself. His hip and thigh throbbed.

While she downed her pills, he set out a pile of clean towels and shook out the bath mat before turning on the water and waiting until it reached a reasonable temperature.

Once he left her alone in the bathroom, Will

groaned. He couldn't afford to picture her naked with water sluicing over creamy skin and feminine curves. It helped to remind himself the water was also sliding over a lot of black-and-blue skin, not to mention the virulently infected slice on her hip.

He rubbed his hand over hair made stiff by the bar soap and sweat, and leaned against the kitchen counter while he scrolled to his buddy's number.

"Javier? Will Gannon."

"Will? Damn, it's good to hear from you! How are you?"

He downplayed his physical and emotional issues for his former teammate and, as soon as he could, said, "I have a situation. I'm hoping you'll help me out."

As he'd expected, despite jeopardizing his medical license, Javier Sanchez promptly agreed to submit a prescription for a powerful antibiotic in Will's name to a pharmacy in Sedro-Woolley. Will had opted against the one here in Concrete. Better not to be seen so close to home right now.

MADDY WAS CAREFUL not to give away how much she dreaded being left alone. She understood Will's reasoning; in a small pharmacy like the one in town, he'd be recognized. People might wonder why he needed the antibiotics. Better for him to go somewhere only the pharmacist would see his name, and he'd be forgotten the minute he walked away. He'd decided to do a major grocery shop while he was out, too, and he'd pick up some basic clothes for her, as well, even if he had to drive into Burlington, the next town down the highway.

She helped make a list of her sizes and preferences. Somehow she wasn't surprised to learn he wasn't much of a salad eater, but he promised to pick up a long list of fruits and veggies.

Finally, he looked at her, creases deepening between his eyebrows. "We need to get in touch with your contact at the marshal's service. I'll pick up a burner phone while I'm shopping because I don't want to use my own. Might be better if I make the call from a location away from the cabin, too. Let's hope he isn't off taking a two-week vacation."

The struggle to survive had required all her inner resources in recent days. His reminder brought it all back in a rush, from the shooting to all the consequences that followed.

"If they really were friends, I bet he'd have ditched his vacation to get back."

Will conceded her point with a dip of his head.

"I guess there's no reason to wait," she said, although she felt a cramp of anxiety. What if Scott was wrong about this friend of his? Who would be more likely to have known the details of his plans for picking her up?

"I remember the Robert part."

"Robert Ruzinski."

"And he's a marshal, too."

"That's what Scott said."

Will kept watching her, making her wonder if she was succeeding in hiding all her worries.

"Do you know something about this Ruzinski?" he asked, confirming her suspicions. "Had you ever heard the name before?"

Maddy shook her head. "All I know is that Scott said to trust him, and no one else."

"Okay." He didn't move. "What's worrying you?"

"Can we really trust anyone in the marshal's office?"

After seeming to ponder he said, "I don't think we have a good alternative. You seem to have trusted Rankin."

Past a lump in her throat, she said, "Yes."

"Then I think we need to keep trusting him. Our only alternative is to turn to the Seattle PD detectives who worked the crime."

"What about the FBI?"

"Would they even have jurisdiction?"

"The fact that Torkelson was up to be a federal judge might give them the excuse they need," she suggested.

"That's true." Will hesitated. "Your call."

Maddy remembered the awful last moments with Scott, the way his fingers had bit into hers. His intensity. The moment when his hand fell away.

He'd called Robert Ruzinski a friend as well as a fellow US marshal. His dying words were, *Trust him.* How could she do any less?

She had to clear her throat. "Let's take a chance on Marshal Ruzinski. Although…won't he want to talk to me?"

"Eventually." Will's voice turned steely. "When I trust him."

She offered a wobbly smile. "I'm so lucky to have you."

He brushed that off, as he had all her thanks. A minute later he pocketed the lists and left, after instructing her to keep the doors and windows locked. He approved her plan to nap.

It was all she could do not to roll her eyes like a teenager. She didn't, because he was all that had stood—and probably still did—between her and an assassin.

The sound of the Jeep engine receded, leaving her in a silence that wasn't as soothing as it should be. She'd been fixed on the single goal of getting out of the mountains where she could recover physically. It was weird now to realize how little thought she'd given to all the future steps. Part of that, it occurred to her, was that she'd had to give her independence, every meaningful choice about her life, even her *name*, into the keeping of the US Marshals Service. She'd had no choice but to become a passive participant in the plans. Once in Everett, Scott would have set up meetings with the prosecutorial team, arranged for transportation to the courthouse, armed escort inside. Now…

How could she safely meet with this Ruzinski? What would he want from her? Would Torkelson's minions dare attack her when she arrived at the courthouse? And…what would she *wear*?

Even knowing how silly it was to obsess over

something so unimportant, she looked down at the navy blue sweatpants that stayed up only because of the drawstring, and that she'd be tripping over if she hadn't rolled up the legs half a dozen times. No panties beneath, and no bra until she could wash both. T-shirt sized for a man with formidable shoulders, which meant it swamped her and hung to midthigh.

She could hardly stop by her apartment—former apartment?—to pick up suitable clothes and heels for her court appearance. She didn't dare call her mother and have her mail an appropriate outfit.

Humor came to her rescue as she tried to imagine Will shopping at Nordstrom for a stylish business suit.

Surely, if he'd lend her his credit card, she could buy what she needed online.

Chapter Eleven

Will had belatedly realized that he could have accomplished all his errands at Fred Meyer, if only he'd thought to ask Javier to send the prescription here. As it was, he picked it up in Sedro-Woolley, then continued down Highway 20 to Burlington, a small city straddling I-5, the major north-south freeway connecting California, Oregon and Washington to Mexico on one end and Canada on the other.

He'd never had a reason to shop for women's clothing, which made this a first. Picking out jeans, shorts, T-shirts and a sweater for Maddy was no problem. Socks and flip-flops, he could handle. The lingerie department was another story. Feeling conspicuous, he struggled to choose a bra and panties. Since he didn't want to linger, he went for items as close as he could get to what she'd been wearing.

He picked up a hair dryer, brush, elastics and gel, too, although he had to wing it where the gel was concerned when he couldn't find the brand she'd suggested. Groceries came next, then the phone with a charger.

Once he'd stowed his bags in the rear of his Jeep, he figured the Fred Meyer parking lot was as good a place as any to charge the phone and make the call.

Frowning as he noticed the time, Will feared the man might have left the office for the day. He might have to try again in the morning.

It took some doing to reach a real human being, but she listened to his request and said pleasantly, "I'll connect you to Marshal Ruzinski, sir."

He got even luckier when his call was answered on the second ring by a brusque voice. "Ruzinski here."

Amazing.

Now was when it got tricky.

Will had decided to go for blunt.

"I'm calling on behalf of Madeline Kane. Marshal Rankin told her to contact you."

The long silence didn't surprise him. Nor did the cagey response.

"What do you know about Ms. Kane?"

"I'd rather not say yet. Marshal Rankin told her that they had to have been betrayed by somebody within your agency. He said she could trust you. No one else." He paused. "Can she?"

Another silence ensued.

"Give me fifteen minutes," he said abruptly. "I'll call you back."

Satisfied, Will moved the Jeep to the Haggen parking lot half a mile away. He opened the back hatch, rummaged in the bags and came up with a package of Fig Newtons. Good to indulge his sweet tooth while he waited.

When the phone rang, the number that came up was unfamiliar. Will answered with a "Yes?"

"I'm calling from my car using a burner phone. I always keep a few around," Ruzinski said. "Now, tell me what you know."

As uneasy as Will was, they'd made the decision to trust this man. That started now.

"I know that Marshal Rankin had gone to fetch her. They were to stay in Everett, or so he said. She's the prime witness in a trial that starts next week. The small plane crashed in the North Cascades National Park. It broke apart. The pilot was already dead when she found him. Rankin wasn't. He had time to tell her it was a bomb, that she needed to hide."

"She wasn't injured?"

"She was. She has a broken collarbone, humerus, possibly ribs. She was concussed and had multiple gashes and horrific bruising. She is, however, alive and prepared to testify."

Ruzinski swore softly. "Scott and she just disappeared. He drove over the mountains to get her, and that was it. A chartered plane had disappeared. No one has spotted it. That's all we could learn."

"I can tell you where to find the wreckage and the bodies. It's possible the wreckage has been tampered with—say, proof that there was a bomb wiped out. I doubt there was any reason for them to have done anything to the bodies."

"They?" the marshal echoed.

"Black helicopter, markings covered. It dropped two men wearing camouflage and outfitted with heavy packs and machine guns. It appears their task was to find Maddy and make certain she never made it out of the mountains."

"And how do you know all of this?" Ruzinski asked with deep suspicion.

"I found Maddy," Will said simply. He explained that he'd intended to scavenge from the plane, but the helicopter beat him there. "I've been out of Army Spec Ops less than a year. I'm a medic," he added. "I was up there climbing alone when I saw the plane go down."

He summed up the rest of the story in as few words as possible: the shooting, the ambush laid for them at the Torrent Creek crossing. The multiple days it took him and Maddy to make the trek out because of her injuries.

"Ideally, she should get X-rays," he concluded, "but we can't risk taking her to a hospital. I've… acquired some antibiotics to knock out the infection, which is her first hurdle."

"You want me to find a place for her?"

"No." Any offer like that was off the table. "She'll stay with me."

"Good." The marshal's relief was apparent. "You can keep her until the trial?"

"Yes."

"The prosecutor will want to put her through some prep before then. Let me think about that. I'll need to talk to her, too."

"We can arrange that," Will agreed, having expected the demand.

"I need to know who you are, too."

He was less enthusiastic about this, but had assumed he'd have to put his name out there. He'd worry more if he believed he could be found. He'd paid cash, six months up front, for the cabin, for no particular reason. The owner was a guy in his sixties, a Vietnam War vet who'd recognized what Will was going through the minute he'd seen him. At the moment the only snail mail he received was addressed to "occupant." He paid his bills online. The utility company was his only concern.

"Will Gannon. William Bradley Gannon. I should warn you that everyone from the driver's license bureau to Mastercard thinks I still live in the barracks at Fort Lewis."

"And you don't."

"Nope."

"That's fortunate."

"Do you have a plan yet?"

Ruzinski wanted to start by finding the wreckage. Will did his best to pinpoint the location and added, "The plane did some damage coming down. I'm sure the pilot did his best to reach an elevation with smaller trees to break the force. Should be visible from the air."

"All right. I'll get search and rescue out to find it, and bomb experts to examine what's left of the plane. I'd really like to recover the bodies. Scott and I have been close friends for a lot of years."

Hearing the grief, Will held his tongue.

"I'll speak to the prosecutor, too, but only her. Officially, I heard about a crash, but don't know if it was the plane Scott chartered or not, and if so whether there's any chance of survivors."

"You trust her?"

"I do. She's good. They start jury selection Monday, you know. She seems confident they can convict Mooney—he's the guy who did the hit—even without Maddy's testimony, but Torkelson is another matter. My call will make her day. Maybe even her year."

Will smiled. "You should know that Maddy is a remarkable woman. She told me what happened. I don't think she needs a whole lot in the way of prepping, especially given that she's an attorney herself."

"Never hurts to plan for what the defense will throw at her."

"Only if we can assure her safety."

"Can I call you at this number?"

"Better if we set up a time and I call you."

They settled on two days hence, eleven in the morning.

Call over, Will did some meandering through Burlington until he found a big green dumpster in an alley. He wiped the phone clean with the hem of his shirt, dropped it on the pavement and stomped on it before tossing it in the dumpster.

A glance at his watch told him he'd been gone longer than he'd intended. Urgency to return to Maddy thrummed inside him.

He kept a sharp eye on the rearview mirror during the drive and, because there were several cars behind him when he reached Concrete, he continued on a couple of miles until he could turn into a driveway framed in dense foliage. He waited until he heard no traffic, backed out and got back on the highway, eastbound now. No one was behind him; no one appeared interested when he turned off the highway this time.

MADDY HAD NO warning before the front door opened. Her heart came close to stopping. She hadn't heard Will's Jeep—her gaze swung wildly. She could go out the back door—

"Maddy?" he called.

"Will?" His name came out in a near whisper.

Apparently too quiet, because he roared, "Maddy?"

"Here!"

He strode into the kitchen and his eyes locked on to hers. His face had been honed by some tension. "You scared me," he said.

"I didn't hear your Jeep. I thought—" Without thinking, she flew into his arms.

They closed hard around her. "Log walls are good insulation."

"Oh," she mumbled against his chest. "I'm sorry, I—"

"Hell with it," he interrupted.

When she lifted her head in surprise, his mouth closed over hers, hot and hard. The kiss seemed to explode. His tongue drove into her mouth and she met it with her own. Her body became hypersensitive.

Her palm rested on his chest and she felt the hammer of his heart. His hand wrapped her hip, his fingers digging into her buttock. The ridge against her belly had her rocking, pushing herself up on tiptoe as if she was climbing him. He nipped her lower lip and she did the same to him. He broke the kiss long enough for them both to gasp for air and then bent to reclaim her mouth.

Or so she thought. The heat in his eyes didn't diminish, but they narrowed slightly. She saw his internal struggle on his face. Finally, he rested his forehead against hers.

"Damn. I didn't mean to…"

His withdrawal stung. She didn't want to hear why he shouldn't have kissed her.

Maddy lifted her hand away from his chest and stepped back. Given no choice, he let his hands drop. They stared at each other for a searing moment. Maddy was overwhelmed by everything she felt: desperate passion, an unfamiliar bone-deep hunger, light-headedness, an echo of the fear that a stranger had entered the house, and so much anger.

"You've been through so much," he said slowly.

"Think of the damage you might have done," she said, her flippancy slicing like a knife. She hoped. "With me so enfeebled and all."

"You've had a raging fever for days," Will snapped. He sounded really mad. "Broken bones. And me? I was about to set you on the table and—" Color streaked the jut of his cheekbones.

For an instant all she saw was herself, stripped of

the sweatpants—and that wouldn't have been hard to do, especially since she had no panties beneath them—lying back on the kitchen table, legs spread. Will standing between them, ripping at the snap and zipper on his jeans…

She blinked a couple of times. She'd melt where she stood if she let herself take the fantasy any further at all.

As an excuse to turn away from him, she opened the refrigerator and grabbed a soda. "Forget about it." Without letting herself look at him, Maddy went to the living room and plopped down on the sofa. There was only silence behind her.

Will took his time but did follow her. Instead of going to his usual spot at the other end of the sofa, he handed her a pill bottle and then chose a chair.

"Quicker you start on these, the better."

"I hope they work fast."

"I talked to Ruzinski."

"He believed you? I mean, about me?"

"He had to. I knew too much." Will reported most of the conversation virtually verbatim, or so she guessed from shifts in intonation.

"So he didn't want to put me in a safe house or something."

"No, I think he was relieved to be able to leave you with me. Who could he trust? I blindsided him. Now he has to look at everyone in his office and wonder."

"Unless jury selection drags, I should be testifying

next week." She could hardly believe the time had really come.

"They sound like they're on schedule."

"Wait, didn't you buy groceries?"

"Crap!" He shot to his feet and jogged out the front door. "What am I thinking?"

HE'D LET A stew of lust and fear, frustration and anger do his thinking for him, that was what.

Damn, he loved kissing her, but he was still brooding when the two of them sat down to dinner. He'd fallen on her like a rabid wolf. He was still ticked that she'd taken offense at his apology. Had he *ever* discounted her intelligence or her strength? No. So what was her problem? He hadn't been rejecting her! All she'd had to do was look at him to see how aroused he was.

Will tried to shut down that kind of thinking. His meal sat untouched in front of him. Maddy was talking, wondering if she could safely call her parents.

"I don't know," he said. "We'd better ask Ruzinski. If there's any chance their phone has a tap on it…"

"But all that would give them is a phone number, right? If I use one of those prepaid phones, how could that hurt?"

Surprised, he said, "Your parents still have a landline?"

"Well…they did a year ago."

"I doubt they'd have dropped it given that they're

probably desperate to hear from you," he said thoughtfully.

"I'm sure they wouldn't."

She looked so eager, Will hated to shake his head, but he did anyway. "We're talking to Ruzinski Saturday. After a year…"

Maddy made a face. "What's another day anyway?"

A few bites later Will said, "You're close to your parents?"

"Yes. Less so to my sisters, just because our lives have diverged." She frowned at him. "What about you? You haven't mentioned your mother. And is your dad still in California?"

"Mother took off when I was ten. She called and sent birthday cards, that kind of thing, for a few years, but the intervals got longer and eventually…" He shrugged. The hurt had dulled to nothingness, but the contrast to her family life held its own brand of pain. "My father is still in the same run-down, single-wide trailer planted on a piece of dirt in a park with a couple of rows of others just like it. No," he corrected himself, "some look worse, but a few have a woman who likes to have flowering baskets or even tries to grow roses. Nobody living there has any money or the slightest hope of that changing. They get by."

Maddy listened with crinkled brow and eyes that showed compassion. "Do you see him?"

"Sure." Will smiled crookedly. "We get along,

more or less. I just didn't want to stay in the area. Too easy never to leave."

"I understand that." Her smile betrayed something he didn't understand. "I guess I never really tried to leave home."

"You went to Stanford."

"Then came back to Seattle. Safe in the nest." As if to end the conversation, she pushed back her chair and rose with her dirty dishes in hand.

He didn't let her reach the sink before he shoved back his chair violently. "That's ridiculous! Our lives were *nothing* alike. Why wouldn't you want to stay close to home?"

She set down the dishes then faced him. "That's what I always told myself, but you make me wonder if I shouldn't have…stretched a little more. You know?"

"You're trying to turn this around," he accused.

"What do you mean?"

Will would swear she was genuinely puzzled. He just shook his head. He didn't have to remind her that her life had changed in a big way this past year. She'd *stretched*, all right, to survive a plane crash and a grueling trek out of the mountains.

EITHER THE CONVERSATION at dinner or the kiss had changed something between her and Will. Clearly, he was ashamed of his background, but call her naive, because she couldn't see why. All she knew was that he'd been keeping his distance in the past day and a half. So obviously so, she'd retreated, as well, not talking much or even looking at him when he was likely to notice.

Maddy's stress level would have been climbing anyway. Her appearance in the courthouse was barely a week away, if that. Did the defense have a clue that anything was wrong? Or had the man paying them have hinted that oh-so-conveniently she wouldn't be able to appear?

No, she didn't want to believe that. The firm hired to defend hit man Kevin Mooney was a respectable one, so far as she knew. One of the associates was a friend of Maddy's from law school. If they understood that the major prosecution witness had been threatened or killed to prevent her appearance, surely they would have refused to continue defending Mooney.

On Friday Will left CNN running all day long, although he jumped channels when local news came on. As tense as she felt, she became a news junkie right alongside him. At least the local politics gave them something impersonal to talk about during meals.

That, and her delight that her temperature was normal after only twenty-four hours on the antibiotic. Much of her headache and general achiness went away with the fever.

The evening local news featured the discovery of a Cessna Skyhawk that had crashed in the North Cascades National Park. Maddy straightened, clutching her broken arm, her gaze riveted to the television.

A news anchor, tone grave, said, "We've received

confirmation that this is the plane reported missing after departing on a charter flight out of a small airfield near Republic in eastern Washington." Footage of the short runway and the hangars flashed on screen before returning to the solemn news anchor. "Authorities also confirmed that they have recovered two bodies from the wreckage, one of whom was the pilot." He talked about Bill Potter and there was a brief interview with his grieving wife. Finally, the anchor concluded by saying, "Authorities are withholding the name of the second victim, likely because they haven't yet been able to notify the next of kin."

The anchors behind the news desk talked briefly about how shocking it was that it had taken so long to locate the plane after the pilot's wife raised the alarm. This was one of the risks taken when the pilot didn't file a flight plan, they agreed.

One turned brightly to the camera. "Next, we'll be talking to—"

With a stab of his thumb, Will turned off the television.

Maddy wanted to feel numb. The crash had happened a week ago. She'd *been* there. *Bang.* Watching in horrified incredulity as the propeller slowed, stopped turning. Still staring at the darkened TV screen, she saw the surreal scene when she regained consciousness and discovered herself to be hanging upside down. The blood dripping from her sliced hand. The struggle on the steep mountainside to find pieces of the plane. Bill Potter. Scott—

She swallowed and closed her eyes. No, she wasn't numb, even though at the same time it all felt unreal, as if it was part of a movie they'd been watching.

"Are you all right?" Will asked quietly.

A cushion separated them on the sleeper sofa that had seen better days.

"Yes. It's just…" Just what? She shook her head.

"They aren't still lying out there waiting to be found."

Typical Will, to sound so gentle even though he'd been remote since yesterday.

"No." She was squeezing the hand emerging from the splint and sling. "I'm glad." When he didn't comment, she turned toward him. "There was nothing about a bomb."

"I'm going to guess the 'authorities'—" he smiled crookedly "—are withholding a few tiny details. It's also possible, as I told Ruzinski, that the men who dropped from the helicopter did some housekeeping, so to speak."

"It would have been hard to be thorough given how far-flung the pieces were." She was proud of how coolly she said that. As if she hadn't been part of the debris. Hadn't seen how violently the pieces of the small plane had been distributed.

To her astonishment, Will reached out and laid his hand over hers. "You're going to hurt yourself."

"What?" She glanced down. "I'm okay."

"No, you're not." He shifted over to the middle cushion and wrapped his arms around her.

For a moment Maddy stayed stiff. He'd been so

clearly determined *not* to touch her; why was he doing this?

But temptation overcame her. No, she wasn't all right. *She* was about to shatter, and heaven knew where the debris would fall. It had to be the sitting and waiting, almost worse than everything that had come before. With a gasp she fitted herself against his solid body, laid her cheek on his shoulder where she'd so often found shelter during their days fighting to survive. She even let herself slide her unbroken arm around his torso. Except for clenching his shirt in her hand, Maddy collapsed.

She didn't cry, didn't even feel the urge. She needed human contact, that was all—except she knew better. She needed Will. She felt dumb now, having dreamed he felt something for her, that maybe in the future they could explore having a relationship. Well, his recent cool distance told her clearly that wasn't happening, but if he offered comfort, she'd accept it.

They stayed like that for a long time. Maddy focused on his steady breathing, the strength enclosing her, until she felt ready to stand alone again.

Then she carefully withdrew, smiled pleasantly without quite meeting his eyes, and said, "I can relax a little bit when we have a plan. Fingers crossed Marshal Ruzinski *has* one."

"Anxious to get back to your life?"

Maddy had a one-shoulder shrug down pat. "Something like that. It would be good to get an X-ray and maybe even a real cast, to start with."

"I'll second that."

When she headed for the bathroom, he stayed where he was. She had a feeling that a brooding gaze followed her.

Chapter Twelve

Will didn't like making the call from his house, but he liked even less the idea of taking Maddy anywhere. She'd have to go out eventually, but right now it wouldn't surprise him if men weren't still cruising Highway 20, maybe asking questions anywhere they could. They might well know that a guy who seemed to be alone in a Jeep had stopped at the eatery in Rockport and bought three cheeseburgers, all with fries, and two drinks.

If they knew that much, it meant Will should stay home, too.

In the end, he chose the better of two options, neither of which made him happy. It helped that Maddy had believed wholeheartedly in Scott Rankin, and Will had gotten a good feeling about Ruzinski in their initial conversation.

So Saturday he and Maddy sat on the back deck overlooking the creek, water splashing over rounded rocks. The shade of the trees, a mix of deciduous and evergreen, kept the deck cool even with midday approaching.

Ruzinski answered on the second ring.

"Will Gannon again."

"Good. Do you have her with you?"

"I do."

"May I speak to her?"

"Sure." Will handed over the phone.

"Marshal Ruzinski? I'm Maddy Kane. I... I want to tell you how sorry I am your friend died protecting me. He was really good to me." She listened for a minute, then said, "Almost the last thing he told me was your name. He called you a friend and said to trust you."

Quiet for another minute or two, she blinked a few times, trying to keep herself from crying if Will was any judge. Finally, she nodded. "Sure. We can put the phone on speaker."

Will took it from her and did so, laying it on the rustic cedar table between their chairs. "Marshal, I'm hoping you can tell us what was found at the crash site. We saw the news, with no mention of bombs or US marshals."

"And we want to keep it that way," he said immediately, "until the trial if at all possible. Ah...investigators found enough remnants of the bomb to verify its existence. They aren't yet sure whether it was triggered by a timing device or a signal sent from the ground."

Will reached over the table for Maddy's hand. She grabbed on tight.

"If it was a timing device, that means they knew how long it would take for the plane to pass above inaccessible country," Maddy said. She succeeded in sounding matter-of-fact, as if the explosion and crash of the Cessna were mildly interesting, how it was brought down an intriguing puzzle. As if she hadn't known the dead men, hadn't been injured, never had nightmares about the moment when the plane fell. Only the strength of her grip on Will's hand said otherwise. "What if the pilot had circled to show me something scenic and we'd come down where there were plenty of people to see and come running?"

"Well, there aren't a lot of those in that country, but at this time of year, Ross Lake and Diablo would have been busy, so yeah, that would have been risky from the bombers' point of view. That's one reason we suspect a radio signal was sent."

"Someone could have been hanging around at a picnic area or campground by either lake," Will agreed. "Watched the plane pass by overhead, waited until he knew it was almost to the Picket Range, where no more than a handful of climbers were likely to be near." He paused. "If I were them, I'd have had a timer on the bomb, too, in case they *didn't* see it."

"That's our assumption," Ruzinski agreed.

"You know that Scott surprised me with the flight over the North Cascades because he thought I'd enjoy it, don't you?" Maddy asked.

"I did know," Ruzinski said after a moment.

"If there's any possibility someone triggered the bomb from Diablo or Ross Lake, that means they knew his intentions, too. That's…not the kind of thing that would have been in a file."

"No, it isn't," the marshal agreed, a hard, angry note in his voice. "He had other friends in the office. Scott was well liked. I can't see him telling many people, though. It's not real pleasant right now, when I have to wonder about everyone I see."

Will leaned forward. "You aren't there right now, are you?"

"Of course not. I'm sitting on a park bench." He paused. "Just so you know, we take pride in having never, in our history, lost a protected witness who followed the guidelines. I don't believe a marshal betrayed Scott and you. He could have been overheard talking, had his phone tapped… I don't know, but you can be damned sure I'll find out."

Will believed him.

Ruzinski cleared his throat. "In the meantime, I have no choice but to turn to the FBI for additional security getting you to the courthouse."

"Who knows that Maddy is alive and still prepared to testify?" Will asked.

"Only the lead prosecutor, Cynthia Yates, and the special agent in charge at the Seattle FBI office. The three of us have agreed to keep the information close. Ms. Kane—"

"Maddy, please," she interjected.

He continued, "Maddy, Ms. Yates wants to meet you in person to discuss your testimony and what the defense might throw at you. All she's telling the others in her office is that she's confident that, with the evidence they have, Mooney will be convicted."

Will mulled that over. If that was true, why risk Maddy to put her in the witness box? Despite his doubts, he decided not to voice them for now.

"How are you doing physically?" Ruzinski asked. "I'm trying to think how we can get you into an ER."

"I'm much improved." She sounded as determined as ever. "The antibiotic is working. My bruises and gashes are healing, although my face may still scare people."

"That's fine by me," he said.

She laughed. Will felt a clutch of serious pride in her. No thugs, however lethal, could stop her.

"Where's the judge?" he asked.

"Torkelson? He was arrested based on what Maddy told the detectives, but he walked out on bail within twenty-four hours, of course. No surprise, he's denying the accusation to anyone who'll listen. He looks real noble when he talks about his long career standing up for justice and the law."

Maddy didn't quite hide a faint shudder.

"Mooney?"

"Still behind bars. The detective in charge of the investigation feels confident he has him solid. Stupid of him to have kept his gun. Of course, it will be open and shut when you testify that you saw his face. From what I hear, Detective Saunders and Ms. Yates have been trying to flip Mooney. He's been offered a tempting deal if he'll name the man who hired him, but so far Mooney has stayed mum. He likely knows about the plan to knock you out, Ms. Kane. Er, Maddy. If you hadn't been able to testify, Torkelson would have a good chance of wriggling out of this. Mooney might be afraid of him, or has been offered a different kind of deal. Once he sees you walk into that courtroom, he may see things a little differently."

"We can only hope." She gazed toward the creek and the leaves dancing in a breeze. "I won't be safe until Judge Torkelson is convicted."

"Right now all we can do is take the next step."

"And what is that, Marshal Ruzinski?"

"Sitting down with Cynthia."

The two men plotted a meet, Will hating even the idea of it but understanding the necessity. The location was theoretically secure. He'd borrow a vehicle; he and Maddy would come up with a disguise for her. Cynthia Yates would walk into her office building as usual but leave surreptitiously with some help from an FBI agent.

At the end Ruzinski said, "Use this number if you need me. Otherwise, we can connect again after you've met with Cynthia Yates."

Maddy said hurriedly, "I'm wondering if I can call my parents."

The pause lasted long enough to tell her what he was going to say. "I'd rather you didn't. I know it's hard on them and you, but remember that they never knew where you were taken or that the plane crash had anything to do with you, so they aren't suffering any new anxiety. They don't expect you to reappear until you're scheduled to testify."

"I know that, but…"

"Somebody may be watching them. If they see open joy and relief, they'll know you're alive and secure enough to be able to call."

She opened her eyes, but he kept talking, sounding regretful. "I don't think we can rule out the possibility of an assault on them in an attempt to find out your whereabouts. Unfortunately, my resources are too limited to allow me to put a 24/7 guard on them."

"And if you did, anyone watching would know why you had."

"I'm afraid so."

"Okay," she conceded.

With the call over, Maddy mentioned her need for an outfit to wear to court. "I'm hoping you have a credit card I can use," she said tentatively. "Of course I'll pay you back once—"

"Don't be ridiculous," Will said curtly. What had she thought, he wouldn't loan her a little money? Or did she suspect he might be flat broke, maybe not even qualifying for credit? That thought irritated him even more. "All you had to do was ask."

"Why are you mad?" Her expression was not friendly.

"I'm not mad."

"You are."

"I'm not—" He cut himself off. Clinging to his pride was one thing; childish behavior another altogether. Will squeezed the back of his neck. "I have plenty of money to lend you whatever you need."

Her glare became bemusement. "I never doubted you do. Why would you think…?" She gave a disgusted huff. "I suppose this is more of the 'I'm servant class, you're privileged' crap."

He stared at her. "Crap?"

"I could call it worse."

His lips thinned, but he shook his head. "No need. You're right. I stumble over my pride occasionally."

"With everyone?" She tipped her head. "Or is it just me?"

"With—" Damn, he had to be honest. "Mostly you," he admitted.

"But…why?"

He'd either hurt her feelings or she was just flat-out perplexed. A burn under Will's breastbone told him he needed to bare himself. God knows she'd trusted him enough times.

"Because you've gotten to me." He sounded hoarse, and wanted really badly to look away from her wide, astonished eyes. "It's hard to imagine a woman with your background and education would have any interest in an unemployed former soldier with a bum hip and leg."

"That's how you see yourself?" She stared at him in obvious bewilderment. "That's ridiculous! Anyway, you said you plan to go to medical school."

"I didn't say *plan*," he corrected her. "I said I'll be applying. But you must know what the competition is like. I may not be accepted anywhere. Then I'll get a job like any other grunt."

Maddy's expression changed. He didn't like to think that was pity he saw.

"You expect to fail?"

He hesitated. Truth was, he'd always been a pretty cocky guy. Mostly, he did believe in himself. It was Maddy who scared him. She was class, he was—

Yeah, that wasn't like him, and he didn't enjoy the feeling.

"No," he said. "I have top-notch grades. I'm hoping the on-the-job experience as a medic makes up for the fact that my degree isn't from a blue-ribbon university. I've been studying hard, and I'm doing really well on the practice MCATs I've taken."

The Medical College Admission Test was notoriously tough, so yeah, he was proud of himself.

Her expression warmed. "They'll be impressed because getting a degree was a lot harder for you than for the typical kid who goes straight off to a four-year school with mommy and daddy paying the tuition." Her forehead crinkled. "You won't be able to start for another year, though."

He rolled his shoulders. "Rehab took everything I had. Then there was the hit of being invalided out of the service. You know it can happen, but that doesn't mean you're prepared. I needed time to… reintegrate, too."

She nodded.

The silence that followed wasn't a comfortable one, even for her, Will thought. Maddy didn't look at him, which had him feeling sick. She hadn't reacted to what he'd said about his feelings for her. Somehow they'd ended up talking about his ambitions instead.

He needed to let it lie. She was stuck with him for the foreseeable future. Why put her on the spot and make their relationship awkward? He'd done enough damage by backing away.

He started to stand. "I'll make sandwiches for lunch."

Maddy laid her hand atop his on the arm of the Adirondack chair. "No, wait. I…have something to say first."

MADDY DIDN'T EVEN know why she felt so shy, but she did. Maybe because Will wasn't like any man she'd ever dated. She'd never felt like this, either. And yes, he'd hurt her each time he withdrew. But she couldn't let this chance pass by. He'd told her how he felt, and she could do that much, too.

Of course, her cheeks were probably flaming red.

His eyes met hers. She knew he wasn't calm only because the muscles in his forearms were rock hard, tendons and veins standing out as did the small bones on the backs of his hands.

"I knew you were attracted to me." Maddy knew her smile was a flop. "I couldn't understand why since I've looked pretty awful since we met with me holding you at gunpoint." She lifted her finger-tips to gingerly touch the side of her face that had been a mass of bruises and cuts. She was healing, but knew fading colors and scabs remained. *Okay, quit procrastinating.* "What you said, um, implies a lot more than that."

"I meant to."

Wincing at his flat tone, she gathered her courage. "Well, I'm interested in you, too, and that's true whether you get into medical school or not. I just never thought you—" Words died as she watched his shifting expression.

"Why?" His puzzlement was plain.

"Oh, come on! I know I've been a burden. And do you have any idea how guilty I feel? You've risked your life for me, over and over. And even though you've been really nice about it, I assumed you'd be glad to unload me as soon as you could."

He swallowed. "I've been dreading the day you leave. I keep telling myself I like being alone, but that's a lie. You…brought me back to life."

"Oh, Will."

She started to rise. So fast she didn't see it coming, Will scooped her up and sat back down with her in his arms. His mouth found hers, both of them made clumsy by need, but it didn't matter. They bumped noses, clanked teeth, but finally found the right angle and the kiss became astonishing: urgent but tender, too; sweet even as need rose. Each time they needed to breathe, they'd look into each other's eyes.

Eventually, a groan rumbled in his chest and she felt a tremor in the hands cradling her head.

"I want you so damn much, but we can't do this. And please don't get mad at me."

Mad? Oh. He'd said the same another time, and she'd stupidly felt rejected.

"I really do feel a lot better overall. If that's what you mean."

Eyes as dark as charcoal searched her face. "You can't tell me you don't still hurt."

No, she couldn't, but today it had been mostly when she got careless in how she moved. "We could, well, find a way." Now her face burned. "Except I'm not on birth control."

"That I can take care of. But…you're serious?"

Maddy squirmed a little for the pleasure of rubbing herself against his powerful thigh, not to mention the ridge against her hip. "I can't think of anything in the world I'd rather do," she confessed.

The sound he made inhuman, Will surged to his feet holding her as if she didn't weigh a thing. He strode across the deck, shoved open the French door with one shoulder and carried her into the living room where he came to a stop.

"Damn. The sofa bed is miserable."

It wasn't so bad for her, probably because she did weigh a lot less than he did but also because she draped herself over him when they slept. Right this minute she didn't think she'd so much as feel the bar that seemed to be right beneath their hips.

"I can climb up to the loft."

"Do you need the bathroom?"

Maddy laughed at his chivalry, unromantic as it was. "No, I'm good." Then she frowned at him. "You didn't say whether you have condoms."

"Picked 'em up when I shopped on Thursday." He crossed the living room in two or three strides and set her on her feet halfway up the steep staircase to the loft. As she climbed, Will kept a hand on her butt, either to boost her or because he was gently squeezing and enjoying it.

He wasn't the only one.

Under a pitched roof, the loft had the same wood floors that could use a refinishing, a queen-size mattress and springs that sat on the floor, a dresser, a small wood stool that obviously served as a bedside stand and a low bookcase.

Within moments Will had yanked the thin blanket and top sheet from the bed. "Maddy. Are you sure?"

She nodded shakily.

"Then lift your good arm." As he had other times, he carefully removed her T-shirt, leaving her breasts bare. Staring, he cupped her breasts to gently rub until she moaned and arched. Still without looking away, Will ripped his shirt over his head and tossed it away before reaching for the button at her waist. He peeled her chinos and panties down her legs, Maddy stepping out of them and her flip-flops at the same time.

Squatting, Will wrapped his hands around her ankles and slid them up. She shivered when he reached the sensitive skin behind her knees. Her breath hitched when calloused fingers stroked over the inside of her thighs. He leaned forward, breathing in her essence, kissed her and then exploded to his feet. Maddy vaguely heard the twin thuds as his shoes hit the floor or walls, who knew? His pants and stretch boxers were gone as fast.

Maddy reached for him and splayed her fingers on his chest. He was…spectacular, those long muscles well-defined, his belly flat and hard. While he stood completely still, she bent forward to rub her cheek against the soft hairs on his chest and explore his contours with her fingertips, finally licking the small hollow at the base of his throat, just because it was there and looked so vulnerable.

He tried to take over then, lifting her and laying her back on the bed before he came down beside her. Always so careful not to hurt her. Knowing he'd never forget made something squeeze hard in her chest. He kissed her breasts and drew each nipple in turn into his mouth, the suction compelling her hips to rise. She wanted his weight on her, to be able to wrap her legs around his waist, feel him deep inside her. Maddy struggled to remember why he still held himself separate.

Her wandering hand touched thick scar tissue. Will returned to kissing her, but she pushed him. "Wait! I need to see—"

"What?" He lifted away in confusion, but Maddy was focused entirely on the scars, some surgical, some from torn flesh, that covered his right hip and reached down his thigh.

She'd known, but seeing it was different. "Oh, Will," she whispered. She stroked the damaged area before looking up in chagrin. "Does that hurt? When I touch you?"

"No." He sounded ragged but cleared his throat. "To tell you the truth, the skin is mostly numb there."

"Oh." She lifted her hand.

He captured it and laid it back where it had been. "Touch me. Anywhere you want. I like it."

"Me, too. I mean—"

Will grinned. "I know what you mean."

Maddy loved what the smile did to that craggy, scarred face. She loved the way he touched her, too, and kissed her, and whispered how beautiful she was even as he had to work around her splinted arm, broken collarbone and gashes. She could hardly wait for the day when she didn't look like she'd been in a plane crash.

She saw him grope beneath the stool and come up with a packet. Lost to sensation, she rubbed against him, hardly aware he was putting the condom on.

Will suddenly rolled to his back and displayed his upper body strength by picking her up again and turning her to straddle him. Eyes betraying desperation as great as what she felt, he said, "Let me know if you hurt."

Hurt?

She took him in, riding him, grateful that he helped pace her with his grip on her hips. Sounds she didn't even recognize kept escaping her. When pleasure seized Maddy, she cried out Will's name— and heard her own as part of a groan when his body bucked as if he had no choice but to follow her.

Chapter Thirteen

The next day after dinner, Maddy sank onto the sofa and cuddled up to Will. "Happy?"

Closing his arm around her, he said, "I'm happy." Which was a major understatement. "You?"

"Of course I am." But her very stillness spoke of the black cloud that hung over them both. This was Wednesday. A week from now or less, she'd be testifying. "Except... I wish we didn't have to do that thing tomorrow," she added.

The *thing*. Drive almost a hundred miles to Bellevue, where the prosecutor would meet them at a borrowed house. Will would have liked it better if they'd planned to meet halfway in between Seattle and Concrete—Everett came to mind, since that was where Scott Rankin had intended to hide Maddy until the trial. But Cynthia Yates had claimed an extremely busy schedule that allowed no time for long drives. Admittedly, in a matter of days she would be starting jury selection for a major trial. She had also refused to do the witness prep over the phone, claiming she never went to trial with a witness she hadn't met with, face-to-face. She sounded annoyed that Maddy had been yanked into hiding before they had a chance to talk.

Will didn't get the feeling she took the danger to Maddy anywhere near seriously enough, but Maddy's determination to do what was asked of her hadn't faltered despite his frustration and fear. This was the first time she'd expressed any worry, although he had been well aware that she wasn't either blithely certain of her safety or in complete denial. He'd awakened her from two or three nightmares a night. She was trying to hold in all her stress.

"If anyone knew where I am," she said slowly, "we'd know."

Translation: they'd be dead.

"So there's no reason the drive should be a problem," Maddy continued. "I don't really see why we even need to switch cars."

They had both been enjoying an interlude. It was time to lay out his biggest worry to her. If everything turned to shit, he needed to know she'd follow orders and react fast.

So he said, "I agree. I don't think we'll be followed. My real concern is that Yates will be. These guys knew she was prosecuting this case long before she walked into the courtroom today. I did some research on Torkelson. You know he was a prosecuting attorney himself before he was appointed to the bench? He knows how it works, how she thinks."

Her muscles tightened. "They're watching *her*. That's what you're saying."

"Yeah." Lay it out there, he told himself. "The judge in particular would know she always meets with witnesses before putting them on the stand. It's unrealistic to believe she can get out of the building unseen. Even if there's a parking garage, they could put people in it watching for her. Even in the building itself. I had the feeling Ruzinski didn't like this plan, either, but felt we had to cooperate."

Maddy pulled away from him, turning on the sofa and tucking one leg under her so she could see his face. "Really? I didn't get that."

"I didn't have the impression you were paying much attention."

Obviously chagrined, she said, "You're right. I wasn't offered a voice in making the arrangements, you know. Still, I should have listened."

"You had a lot to think about." He leaned forward to kiss her lightly, then smiled. "It's also possible he was chafing at having to turn to another agency to do what he can't."

Maddy chuckled. "It can't be comfortable for him to have to admit the marshal's service needs help protecting a witness under *their* care."

"Nope."

He waited while she thought it over. "So we're just going to walk—drive—into a potential ambush?"

"I'll approach with great care. You need to be ready to jump when I say jump."

"Haven't I always?"

"Yeah," Will said gruffly. "You have. I have the feeling you aren't usually a docile woman, though, and the better you feel, the more likely you are to want to think for yourself."

Maddy frowned at him. "Thinking for myself doesn't make me stupid, you know."

"That's not what I—"

She cut him off. "I'd have died if it weren't for you. *You've* kept me alive. I promise to jump when you say so."

Will slid a hand around her nape and squeezed. "You're right. I'm sorry. I'm just, uh…"

"Worried."

Scared out of his skull, actually, but he wasn't going to say that. He wouldn't quit being scared even if tomorrow's expedition went like clockwork. The trial had to take place at the courthouse, and he had no doubt at all that they'd be ambushed there. It would be their last chance.

Of course, a second trial was scheduled to begin in late August, and Maddy had to testify in it, too. Will was less concerned about that one, because she'd already have described in court what she saw and heard the day her client was gunned down. Shutting her up after that wouldn't help Judge Torkelson.

Which didn't mean Will intended to relax one iota until Torkelson was convicted and led away in cuffs.

"How about we put it out of our minds for the rest of the day," he suggested.

A smile quivered on her mouth. "That's a lot of hours to fill. I wonder what's on Netflix?"

"Netflix isn't quite what I had in mind." Will traced the curve of her lips with his forefinger. When she nipped it, his body jolted. "You know, the fit is tight here if we don't pull out the bed, but if I spoon you from behind..."

Just like that, he was painfully aroused. And even more so when he saw her eyes darken and her lips part.

"That sounds interesting," she said huskily. "I'm betting you don't have a condom handy, though."

With a groan, he let his head fall back. Then he eased himself to his feet. There was no way around it. "Close your eyes, count to twenty and I'll be back."

Maddy's chuckle followed him up to the loft.

IT WAS NOT a fun drive.

At least once they were on the freeway and Will was confident they weren't being followed, he let Maddy sit up. Naturally, he'd consigned her to the backseat so that she could dive for cover beneath the familiar blue tarp if need be. She fastened her seat belt, glanced at the back of Will's head and some of his stubborn jaw and angular cheekbone, all she could see, then looked out the window just as they drove over the Skagit River. It was more impressive than she'd have expected, broad and running high, deceptively placid except for the ripples of current.

She could only remember traveling this far north once, when she and Doug had gone to La Conner for a weekend getaway. They'd been chattering, and she hadn't paid that much attention.

Doug. She hardly thought of him. They'd been seeing each other for nearly a year before she witnessed the shooting that changed everything, and yet Maddy could barely picture his face. How much had he been told about her disappearance? She wondered how quickly he'd moved on...because she felt sure he would have.

A better question was why she wasted so much time on a tepid relationship.

The freeway briefly followed the river as it looped south before it curved west again. Once Mount Vernon fell behind them, the land was flat and mostly agricultural although she saw a plant nursery, wine grapes and a sign advertising rides in hang gliders.

Maddy was not in any hurry to fly again. *Never* sounded good.

Once they crossed another river, the Snohomish, traffic increased and the surroundings were urban. First Everett, then Lynnwood where Will exited. This was where they'd leave the Jeep and borrow a car from a friend of his for the last leg of the trip.

Will didn't tell her to hide, but he didn't introduce his friend, either. The two talked briefly on the front porch of the modest rambler and the guy handed over the keys with only one curious glance her way. Will carried the tarp to the silver Toyota Corolla and said, "I'm afraid you need to stay in the back."

She got in and shook out the tarp so she could squirm under it quickly. Will drove a circuitous route out of the neighborhood, his gaze turning frequently to the rearview mirror. Apparently satisfied, he got on Highway 405, which led south down the east side of Lake Washington.

The more familiar the sights became, the more nervous Maddy got. She'd grown up in Redmond, bordering on Bellevue. They'd be passing within half a mile of her childhood home. She felt an ache to hear her parents' voices, hug them.

Not helpful.

"We're coming up on the exit," Will said. "I want you out of sight."

"Okay." The tarp crackled as she lay down on the seat and drew it over her. Knowing how close they were, she felt suddenly claustrophobic. "Um...will you talk to me?"

"When I can."

He complained aloud about hitting a red light every block, about the traffic near Bellevue Mall, then grew quiet for a few minutes. "Why here?" he said almost beneath his breath. "Nobody in the prosecutor's office should earn enough to run in these circles."

From that, Maddy deduced that they were still heading straight for the lake. He was right; homes here started over a million dollars. Prices on waterview or waterfront property climbed sharply from there.

Her nerves tightened when he turned at last, and turned again. His phone buzzed.

"Yeah?" A moment later, "We're getting there. I don't like this." He listened again, said, "Okay," then, in an entirely different voice, "You okay, Maddy?"

"Yes. Are we almost there?"

"Yeah. I'm circling a few blocks, mapping the fastest way to get out of here if we need to."

"Do you see anything to worry you?"

"More parked cars than I like. All nice ones. I guess no one here drives an eight-year-old Jeep."

"No, but neither are you at the moment."

"At least this car is still shiny." After a minute he said, "What did you drive?"

"Would you believe a Honda Civic?"

"No BMW or Land Rover?"

She laughed, even though she knew he was trying to distract her from the building tension. "Nope."

The phone buzzed again. Will didn't bother with a hello. He listened, then said, "Be ready."

"Who was that?"

"The FBI agent. That was his all clear."

"But you don't buy it."

He didn't answer. Didn't have to answer.

No, HE WASN'T any more convinced this was safe than he'd been when he and the marshal first discussed it. Will wished he knew whether this FBI Special Agent Moore was seasoned or a rookie. He sounded too casual.

The garages and parking on this block were in the alley running behind the homes. Turning into the alley, Will wished he had eyes in the back of his head. He didn't like being boxed in. He'd have more options if he'd parked at the curb and they'd entered the front door. Moore was right that they'd draw less attention this way—but who cared what the neighbors thought?

The big shiny black SUV parked next to the third garage on the right looked government even if the license plate didn't say so.

His gaze flicked from the rearview mirror to each side mirror, back to the front, then rearview. He wished he was driving a Humvee.

No other vehicles appeared. He braked but didn't turn off the engine. There was zero movement until the garage door rolled up, revealing a parked Lexus and a workbench and lawn mower.

He said quietly, "Don't sit up until I come around the car to let you out. Stay close to me. Got it?"

"Yes."

Leave the key in the ignition, he decided. He didn't pull the emergency brake on, either.

They should have supplied her with a Kevlar vest. Will was angry at himself for not asking. For all they knew, he was unarmed, depending entirely on the single agent who stood inside the garage. He hadn't told Ruzinski that he had the dead marshal's handgun. He'd give it back eventually.

At least Special Agent Moore had his weapon in his hands and appeared alert.

Will's skin crawled as he got out, slammed his door and walked around the front of the Corolla. How many times had he felt this, when he *knew* they were being watched? It was quiet. Too quiet. His every instinct told him to jump back in the damn car and step on the gas. Get out of here. But he acknowledged that his combat senses were still raw. Maybe he wasn't ready to be thrown back into this kind of situation.

Or he should listen to instincts built on experience.

He scanned the entire alley, rooftops, fences. He couldn't relax, but had to open the back door for Maddy to wriggle out, hampered by the arm in a splint and sling.

"Keep low," he murmured.

Her hair ruffled, she crouched next to the fender.

"What's taking so long?" the agent asked from behind him. "Get her in here."

Will ignored him. Talking to Maddy, he said, "All right, scoot behind me and stand up. Put your hand on my back so I know where you are."

She did exactly as he asked.

"We're going to back up," he said in the same quiet voice. "You take a step, wait for me to take one."

Feeling as if every hair on his body bristled, Will heard the soft scrape of her foot moving backward on asphalt. He moved his right foot back, keeping his weight on his stronger side.

"Another—"

A tiny rattling sound was his only warning before the gate almost directly across the alley burst open and a man in black stepped out shooting.

The first shot pinged off the roof of the Corolla and passed within inches of his head.

"Drop!" he yelled.

Maddy did so without hesitation, crawling by him for the shelter of the car.

The second shot came from higher and went over the car. A sharp cry from behind told Will the agent was down.

He started shooting. The closest man jerked and fell forward. Will could barely see the flattened form of the gunman on the roof of a garage they'd driven right past, but he took some shots as he flung open the back door for Maddy.

"In, in."

She scrambled, he slammed it and duckwalked around to the back bumper. It was farther from the driver door, and he counted on his choice being unexpected.

One look over his shoulder. Moore had pulled himself to the front corner of the garage where he was partially sheltered by the back end of the Lexus. Blood soaked one thigh of his pants, but he held his gun in firing position. His eyes met Will's.

His lips scarcely moved as he said, "I'll provide cover. Get her out of here."

Crouching, Will counted a few seconds, leaned his head around the bumper for a quick glimpse then came out shooting. And, hell, he had to leap over the prone and unmoving body of gunman number one. Kept shooting until the magazine was empty, leaped into the front seat. Started the engine, thrust the gearshift into Drive and slammed his foot down on the accelerator. The small Corolla rocketed toward the side street.

ALMOST AS SCARED as she'd been when that propeller quit turning, Maddy hated being blind. She heard the door being opened, felt the car rock when Will flung himself in. She kept waiting for another gunshot, to hear a guttural sound when he was hit. The Corolla would swerve, smash into a garage or a parked car. If he was killed—

Don't think it.

How could she not, after he had once again put his body between her and danger? He'd been *prepared* to take a bullet. For her.

The car swayed through another turn, after which she thought it slowed.

"Is anyone following us?" she asked.

"Not yet." Will sounded grim.

Another turn, and she heard his voice.

"Ruzinski." Pause. "Blew up in our face. Two gunmen were waiting. The FBI guy is wounded. Maddy and I got out. Car suffered a lot of damage. I'm looking to ditch it." A long silence. "Yeah, it's missing a couple of windows, got some interesting dents. I'd get pulled over for sure." Then, "Uh-huh, I can do that. Thanks."

Assuming the conversation was over, Maddy asked, "Can I please sit up?"

"I don't see why not. We're going to drive half a mile, a tow truck will pick up the car and Ruzinski is coming for us."

Relief rushed through her as she emerged from beneath the tarp. A mole sniffing the air. "Are you hurt?"

"No. Agent Moore was shot, but should be okay. We'll find out."

Dazed, she said, "You were right."

"I shouldn't have agreed to this in the first place." His steely voice made it plain that his cooperation would be hard won in the future. "We should both have been wearing vests."

"Vests?"

"Kevlar. Bulletproof." He shook his head, his eyes meeting hers in the rearview mirror. "It was a miracle neither of us took a bullet. More so that a tire didn't get shot out."

"Maybe they aren't that smart," she ventured.

"No. I recognized one of them."

"But not the other?"

"He was up on a roof. Couldn't see him well enough."

Her pulse was only now slowing. "They quit shooting." *Are they dead? What will happen to the bodies?*

"The one in the alley was down. I don't know if I killed him or not. The one on the roof… Not sure. Moore and I were both banging away at him. If we pinged him at all, he may have dropped his rifle. The roof was pitched enough, it would have slid away."

And dropped into somebody's yard. Remembering the barrage of bullets, Maddy could only imagine how many bullet holes residents would find in fences and garage siding. And maybe in a roof?

She hadn't been paying attention to their route, but now Will steered into a parking lot at a lakefront park, driving to the far end and backing into a slot so that he could see who was coming.

Then he reached for the gun he must have tossed on the passenger seat, dug in a pocket and changed magazines.

"How many bullets does that hold?" Maddy asked.

He glanced in the rearview mirror again. "Thirteen, one in the chamber. Remind me to give you some basic lessons before our next exciting outing."

Her laugh might have been just a little hysterical. Will grinned because he'd gotten what he had been aiming for.

"Ah, listen." He opened the glove compartment and took something out. "I need to take the license plates off."

"Because they'd lead to your friend," she realized.

"Nope. Because they don't belong on this car." He got out, stuck his head back in and added, "Paul collects license plates. That's one reason I called him. These are BC plates. He'll want them back even if there is a bullet hole or two."

"He's not going to be mad about the car?"

"Nah, he'll get it back in pristine shape. This autobody place does a lot of work for local LEAs."

LEA. She considered that while Will crouched first behind the back bumper then the front. She'd heard the acronym before… Law enforcement agencies. That was it. What, was the guy who owned the shop a retired cop?

Will reappeared in the door. "Ruzinski is here."

They transferred to an older Blazer or Explorer

or something like that. Maddy, of course, was consigned to the backseat. She was beginning to get
annoyed by the assumption she wouldn't have anything worthwhile to contribute. She reminded herself that she'd have her chance when she made it into
the courtroom.

The marshal glanced at the license plates Will
set down by his feet, raised his eyebrows but didn't
comment.

For some reason he didn't look quite like she'd
expected. He was thin, taller even than Will, she
thought, with short blond hair spiked with silver,
and blue eyes. Except for crow's-feet beside those
eyes, his face was as smooth as that of a man decades
younger than she somehow knew he was.

Two blocks away from the park, he glanced at
Will. "I hear you were armed."

"You talked to Moore? Is he okay?"

"Sounds like. Said he bled like a stuck pig."

After a pause Will said, "I was carrying. Did you
really think I'd risk Maddy in a setup like this if I
wasn't?" His voice crackled with anger. "Depending on someone I've never worked with before? Who
was there *alone*?"

"Calm down. I didn't think that. But there is a
dead man in that alley. I need to know where those
bullets came from."

He'd killed for her. And yes, he must have killed
before, but Maddy didn't like knowing this violence
had been committed on her behalf.

"I have Scott Rankin's Glock. Maddy grabbed it for protection," he said tersely.

Ruzinski was quiet for a minute. "I tried to educate myself about your background, but I couldn't learn much but that you were army."

"Delta Force."

The marshal's eyebrows climbed. "On leave?"

Will shook his head. "I'm out. Humpty Dumpty and I have something in common."

"Couldn't put you back together again? Looks like they came close."

"Good enough, but not up to active-duty demands."

"I see."

Delta Force. She'd been even luckier than she knew, Maddy realized. What she couldn't understand was how Will had reconciled being a healer with the violence he must also have committed. It was telling that his goal now was to become a family doctor. He had to be looking for peace, finding a place he could help instead of harm.

And yet he hadn't hesitated to jump into the mess her life had become.

My hero, she thought, knowing quite well what he'd say to her calling him that.

Chapter Fourteen

Will hoped recriminations had been flying between the FBI and the Seattle City Attorney's office. When Yates, who he had learned was a senior deputy prosecuting attorney, called Maddy Thursday evening after the debacle, Will eavesdropped unashamedly, even though he could hear only one side of the conversation. Even so, he could tell that Cynthia Yates started with a shovelful of apologies.

Leaning against the kitchen counter, arms crossed, he watched Maddy's reaction.

From her place at the kitchen table, she rolled her eyes toward Will and said repeatedly, "Thank you, but you don't need to—yes, I understand. No, I don't think we can discount the resources a former judge commands. It does make me nervous about reaching the courtroom safely." She listened some more, expressed more understanding and finally said, "Why don't we just get down to business?"

She had displayed more patience than Will felt. He'd expressed his reservations about the meet loud and clear. Ruzinski claimed to have shared them, but had he really? Who knew?

Apparently, the FBI agent had been discharged from the hospital after only one night's stay but with his femur shattered. He'd be on disability for several months. Will and Maddy would certainly be dead if they had trotted on into the garage as ordered.

Will had never had trouble following orders within his unit, but he'd since had an attitude adjustment. No more.

He didn't listen closely as the two women had an intense discussion about courtroom tactics, what to expect from counsel for the defense and the judge. Maddy had appeared before her on a couple of occasions and had strong opinions on the woman's particular areas of tolerance and, on the flip side, her biases. During this call, Maddy didn't docilely listen; she sometimes argued, sometimes stood firm, sometimes acquiesced. She had strong opinions and didn't back down unless Ms. Yates had solid reasons for a strategy.

The Maddy of today didn't have a lot of resemblance to the injured, feverish survivor of a plane crash, but she hadn't lost the quality that enabled her to survive: determination.

While the women talked, Maddy took extensive notes on Will's laptop, her fingers flying. Watching her, he smiled.

When he heard her say, "I'm going to speakerphone," he tuned in.

"I'm sure you'll be in discussions with the Seattle

PD and courthouse security about your arrival next Monday, but I want to reassure you—"

Will cut the woman off. "We won't be reassured until we've safely reached the courtroom. I'm assuming your office hasn't anything to do with those arrangements?"

"Only in the sense that we're aware of what's happening and offer our assistance where necessary."

"Ms. Yates, I encourage you to take security measures yourself. If you were to be killed, it seems likely the trial would be postponed."

Silence told him he'd surprised her.

"That's possible," she said after a minute. "But postponement wouldn't help the defendant's cause."

"Forget Kevin Mooney. The former judge is clearly a ruthless man who will do anything at all to avoid going to trial. As multiple attacks on Maddy make plain, he wants her dead. A postponement would give him more time to find her."

"Very well," the DA said stiffly. "I'll relocate for the rest of the week and will request personal security until the trial ends."

"Good."

He let the two women wind it up. Torkelson would likely appear before a different judge on his day in court, but this trial could in effect convict him. Considering he'd ordered the original murder to cover up a rape, it was his bad luck that neither he nor Mooney were likely to get much sympathy from the female judge, female prosecutor and female primary witness.

Tough luck.

After Maddy hung up, Will said abruptly, "Are your parents planning to attend the trial the day you're testifying?"

"I'm sure they are."

"If their lives were threatened…"

"I'd do just about anything," she finished, stricken face giving away how hard she'd been hit. "I should have thought of that sooner."

"Somebody should have," he said grimly. "From the minute the marshal's office knew a bomb had brought that plane down, I'd have expected security measures to have been ramped up to DEFCON one. Why hasn't that happened?"

"I…don't know."

"You get a sense of anything off with Ms. Yates?"

"No." She started shaking her head. "No."

"Okay."

Maddy was the one to say, with clear reluctance, "Marshal Ruzinski?"

Will went with his gut. "No. I think he's focused on finding the leak."

"So what? You think Torkelson might have a hold on some police officers? Courthouse security?"

He blew out a breath and scrubbed his hands over his head. "Yeah, I guess I do. The man was a prominent local judge. He could make or break people's lives. It's pretty clear he lacks a conscience or any kind of morality. Sociopaths can be CEOs of a Fortune 500 company…or an attorney or superior court judge. We don't know whether he preyed on just one woman, your client, or whether he's bought off or intimidated a bunch of women. From his point of view, his career and life were going just fine until the one woman decided to speak out. First, he blamed her, then you. I don't trust even round-the-clock security for your parents, I'd like them to fly out tonight. London, the Caribbean, doesn't matter. What's important is that they go off the grid when they get there. Find a place to stay that accepts cash and doesn't insist on getting a name."

The way Maddy had blanched worried Will, but even if he could, he wouldn't take back his suggestion. The stakes were high, the man set on stopping Maddy intelligent and remorseless.

"Let's go for a drive," he said.

Maddy didn't argue.

WILL DROVE ALL the way to Bellingham, not far from the Canadian border, before he pulled into a vast parking lot in front of a shopping mall.

Then he took a phone out of the glove compartment and handed it to her. "Call them."

Maddy nodded.

His steady gray eyes held hers for a long moment before he smiled, bent his head and kissed her. The kiss was quick, but also tender and possessive. She tingled all over by the time he opened his door and got out.

"You can listen if you want," she said.

"You deserve a few minutes with them. Just be sure nobody says anything too specific. I'm calling

Ruzinski." He slammed the door and walked around to the front of his Jeep, where she could see him lifting another phone to his ear. Typically for him, he didn't stand still. He paced with seeming idleness as he talked, but never going far from the Jeep. She had a feeling he was aware of every car in their vicinity that had a person waiting in it, every shopper heading toward the mall entrance or returning to a car with full bags.

He also looked incredibly sexy, his jeans well worn to conform to his butt and the long muscles of his thighs, his brown hair rumpled, strong forearms bared by the T-shirt. Maddy had never been involved with a man who had anywhere near his physical presence.

She gave herself a shake, dialed her parents' phone number and stared down at it for a minute. She'd missed them so much, hated knowing how scared they must have been about her. Then she pushed Send.

"Hello?"

"Mom?"

The sound her mother made might have been a sob. "Maddy? It's you?"

"Yes." When she tasted salt, Maddy realized she was crying. She had to say, "Just a minute," and juggled the phone while she swiped away the tears. "I'm sorry."

Her father must have picked up an extension, because it was him saying urgently, "Maddy? You're all right?"

"I'm fine, Dad." She took a deep breath. "Mostly."

"Mostly?" Mom. "What's that mean?"

"I don't know if you read about the small plane going down in the North Cascades."

They had, and were horrified when she told them about the bomb. She didn't linger on the ordeal getting out of the mountains, but gave a quick summation.

"You know I'm supposed to testify Monday."

"We didn't know what day for sure, but we'll be there."

"No, that's the thing. Will—he's the ex-army Delta Force guy who found me up there and got me safely out of the mountains—he thinks you could be in danger. There have been other attacks. I won't go into that right now, but he wants you to pack and go somewhere tonight. Get on a plane and wherever you go just use cash. It'll only be for a week or two."

After a long pause, her father said, "You're right. We have to remove any chance we could be used to influence you. We could go to—"

"No! Don't tell me. If your phone is tapped..."

She heard her father breathing. Or maybe both of her parents, synchronized.

"Understood," he said finally. "We'll do that. As long as you have someone..."

"I do." Maddy had to clear her throat and repeat the words. "I do. Will has been amazing. I trust him."

Her voice must have softened, because her mother said, "Like that, is it?"

Her lips trembled on a smile. "Yes. Maybe. I don't

know." Her face was wet again. "I love you. Please stay safe."

"You, too," her father said gruffly, and she ended the call.

After mopping her cheeks with the hem of her shirt, Maddy lifted her head to see that Will had come to a stop right in front of the car where he could watch her. She couldn't seem to draw a breath. She could only look at him and hope she wasn't imagining what she thought she saw in his eyes.

And that he didn't take a bullet for her and die.

WILL TOOK HIS time making love to Maddy that night. They could explore each other's body in between quiet talks tonight and every night to come. He pretended the days weren't counting down.

He found Maddy endlessly fascinating, starting with that supple body and feminine curves, with the way she responded to his touch—and the way she touched him.

But it was more than that. He'd liked women he'd been involved with before, but nothing he had felt measured up to this. He wanted to know everything about Maddy. How had a beautiful woman who'd grown up in privilege become so tough and principled? Why did she regret not having broken more of her ties to home? What did she imagine she'd have done with her life if she hadn't become an attorney?

What would she think about moving to Houston or Los Angeles, Cincinnati or Atlanta, depending on where he was accepted to medical school?

Maybe most important, he needed to find out what happened when she was no longer living in fear for her life, depending on him for her safety. She might see him differently then, start noticing that he had an ugly scar on his face and worse ones on his body, that he knew more about primitive living in the bone-dry mountains of Afghanistan than he did fitting in with people his age in a sophisticated American city. She'd discover that he wouldn't have a clue how to pick from a wine list at a fancy restaurant, that most nightlife held no interest to him even if he could stand the crowds and the noise and flashing multi-colored lights.

Deep in his heart, Will didn't believe any of that would make a difference to her. Going through what they had together, he and Maddy knew each other better in barely over a week than most dating couples would in a year or more. Stress and danger did that to you—taught you whether someone had the qualities that meant you could rely on them, now and forever.

With an effort, he pushed all that out of his mind. Their first lovemaking was slow and emotional. Then came fast, even desperate. He woke up once to find her rubbing against him. Come morning, his body spooned hers, and he slid into her from behind for another tender lovemaking. He wouldn't mind waking up like that every morning for the rest of his life.

Getting dressed, starting the coffee and scrambling some eggs while Maddy wrapped a plastic bag around her arm and showered, Will glanced

involuntarily at a calendar that had hung in this
kitchen when he moved in.

Five more days.

THE GOOD NEWS came from Ruzinski, who called Friday to let them know that a clerk in the marshal's office had been arrested for selling info about Rankin's
plans for Maddy. Once accused, the clerk had crumpled and admitted that she'd overheard him talking
to the pilot when he booked the charter. Ruzinski
was confident she'd acted alone.

He also informed them that a female Seattle PD
officer who resembled Maddy enough to pass as
her from a distance agreed to serve as a decoy. She
would be escorted into the courthouse the way a protected witness normally would be. Will guessed there
was a tunnel directly from the jail, or it would be
via a loading dock or something like that. He didn't
ask, and Ruzinski didn't volunteer the information.

Ruzinski did admit to being bothered by the courthouse security liaison's insistence on knowing Will
and Marshal Ruzinski's plans. The guy didn't like it
when Ruzinski refused to share how they intended
to reach the courthouse. It was possible the security
liaison felt he was being kept from doing his job—
but it was also possible he needed the information
for another reason altogether.

Ruzinski and Will had already made the decision
to trust no one. They'd considered calling the detective who arrested Kevin Mooney and would also be
testifying. He almost had to be trustworthy. But there

were risks. He might trust somebody whose integrity had been bought. He wasn't a direct threat to the judge, but his testimony was critical to convicting Mooney. If he and Maddy both were killed, Mooney would walk. No, best if he, too, knew nothing about how Maddy was to get safely into the courtroom.

If Ruzinski and Will didn't involve anyone else, they had two options: take her in through a tunnel from the county admin building across Fourth Avenue from the courthouse, or walk in the main entrance. Either way, they'd have to stand in line like everyone else to go through airport-like security.

Ruzinski liked the first option, Will the second. He'd have to turn in his gun before entering the tunnel, leaving Ruzinski the only one of them armed. If a cop or guard had been turned, the tunnel could be a trap. Put someone ahead, someone behind, and they'd have no escape. Plus, they'd have to get safely into the administration building in the first place.

His suggestion to stroll right in the main entrance might be the most unexpected but had its own downside if they drove themselves. The closest parking lot was a block away. He shook his head at the idea of them standing to wait for lights to change so they could cross streets. At least a *moving* target was harder to hit.

"Better," he had said to Ruzinski, and with Maddy listening in, "we take a bus, a taxi or an Uber. We could be dropped off right in front."

"That's the busiest entrance. There can be long waits until you go through security."

"Maddy isn't likely to testify until afternoon. How much line would there be once the morning rush has passed?"

"She'd stand out less if she arrived at the same time as employees and jurors," the marshal argued.

"Late morning we could get her inside a lot quicker."

"You picturing a disguise?" Ruzinski asked.

"Of course I am. She could be—" His gaze touched on her breasts. Not a man. "An old woman. I'm her dutiful son."

"And I'm the old man," Ruzinski said drily.

Will grinned despite the serious subject. "When the shoe fits."

Maddy laughed.

The marshal grumbled, "Tell her I heard that."

Laughter sparkling in her eyes, she said, "A little hair dye and *he* could be my dutiful son."

"Sure."

"What if we were a trio of old people?" Maddy suggested.

"Why would one witness, juror, whatever, bring two other people along? I think Ruzinski should be arriving separately. Just happen to be ahead or behind us in line."

"I agree," the marshal said. "Crap. You know witnesses who have been threatened are safely brought in and out of the courthouse all the time. Maybe we should trust the usual protocols. Maddy isn't the first one I've worked with who was threatened, you know."

On a bite of anger, Will countered, "So far, she's narrowly escaped death three times, and then there was the ambush we evaded. And the ultimate defendant isn't a crooked businessman or money launderer. He's a superior court judge."

"Was. But you're right. I'm just frustrated. Wait a minute. Could we bring her in by helicopter?"

Maddy must have heard that last word, because her eyes widened, and not in a good way.

All Will had to say was, "Bomb, remember?"

Ruzinski swore.

Maddy spoke up. "One of the men in the alley escaped. They know I have a broken arm. How are we supposed to hide that?"

Good question.

MADDY DIDN'T EVEN hear what the Uber driver and Will were saying. She sat in the backseat of the silver Toyota Prius, gazing out the passenger window at a wet, gray day. Raindrops slid over the glass.

Only a year ago she'd belonged here in downtown Seattle. She might know some of the men in well-cut suits and women in heels carrying umbrellas as they navigated the steep, rain-slicked sidewalks. Her law firm was in the building at the corner ahead. She could go in, take the elevator to the fifth floor and stroll in. Would anyone recognize her in the thick makeup? Would they recognize her without it? How much turnover in personnel had there been in the past year?

She'd always assumed she would go back to work

there, as if the slice of time she'd been away was nothing. Vacation. What she hadn't imagined was the changes in herself she only now began to recognize.

I don't belong.

Her strange mood today might have something to do with the sense of alienation, Maddy recognized. The long-awaited day was here, and she felt fatalism instead of fear. Which might be best, if it didn't slow her reaction time.

Will might be talking to the Uber driver, a prematurely balding young man, but really he was keeping an eye on her.

The rain was a stroke of luck, allowing Maddy to wear a calf-length, enveloping raincoat that hid both the splint on her left arm and the bulky Kevlar vest that Marshal Ruzinski had supplied. With a forest green hooded slicker over his own vest, Will looked thicker through the waist and chest than usual, which fit with his drastically aged face. Meeting him for the first time, Maddy would have sworn he was in his sixties, courtesy of salt-and-pepper hair and lines skillfully applied by the woman who'd done their makeup. Her own face was equally strange to her.

Maybe that last, astonished look in the mirror had given rise to her peculiar mood.

She heard Will say, "I didn't realize the hills were so steep here. Why don't you go around the block so you can drop us right by the entrance? My wife needs hip replacement surgery."

The driver obediently took a left on Cherry Street, his eyes meeting Maddy's in the rearview mirror.

"My dad had the surgery six months ago. I'd swear it took ten years off his age."

Her lips curved on command. "I'm looking forward to not living with constant pain, I can tell you." How true.

"I can imagine."

Two right turns, and they passed the small city park where she'd sat on a bench and eaten lunch a few times during a break from a trial. Almost there. Her pulse jumped.

A last right, onto Third Avenue, and the Uber driver steered them to the curb in front of the main entrance.

Will's phone buzzed. He took it from his pocket, read a text and, expression never changing, held out his phone so she could read it, too.

Decoy under attack. Shots fired.

They thanked the driver and exited onto the sidewalk, Will first then Maddy. He tucked her close to his side, his head turning. The sidewalk was busy despite the rain.

A taxi pulled up behind the Prius and a man got out. Dismissing him, Maddy worried. Where was the marshal?

"We're ready," Will said in a low voice. "Let's move."

Ready? Maddy felt a shock as she sneaked another look at the stranger from the taxi. Not a stranger. Ruzinski.

He didn't so much as glance at them but, as planned, fell in behind them as they started toward the doors.

Maddy had taken only a few steps when she heard a horribly familiar coughing sound. At the same moment somebody bumped her from behind.

Ruzinski had fallen to the sidewalk and wasn't trying to get back up. The gun he must have had in his hand skittered a few feet across the concrete.

Without thinking, she bent to pick it up.

Chapter Fifteen

People screamed and ran, knocking each other over and confusing the scene. Unbelievable that these bastards were willing to gun down innocent passersby. With the assailant using a suppressor, Will had barely heard the first shot. Not until a woman five feet beyond Maddy went down, blood blossoming on her pale blue suit jacket, did Will know shots were still being fired.

That might have *been* Maddy, if she hadn't unexpectedly ducked.

Weapon extended, Will swung in a circle, almost straddling her, waiting for her to rise. Where was the shooter? Damn it, *where*? His gaze flicked from face to face. Men of all ages, several more women. Panhandler...with cold eyes and a handgun spitting bullets. Probably not alone, but one at a time.

Will fired. Once, twice, three times. The gunman slammed back against the gray wall of the courthouse.

"Will!" Maddy screamed.

He spun. The bullet slammed into his chest, dead center. More shots hammered his torso. He reeled, stumbled back. Saw Maddy on her knees, gripping the marshal's gun with both hands, which meant she'd ditched the sling. This shooter wore a black balaclava and leaned out of a taxi that had pulled up behind Ruzinski's.

Will kept pulling the trigger, but he was going down. Leaving Maddy—except she was firing, too, nothing on her face he'd ever seen. God, please don't let her kill an innocent. Don't let her die.

His head hit the pavement and the lights went out.

ASTONISHINGLY, HER HANDS were steady. If there was any pain from her broken arm, she didn't feel it. Maddy aimed low; this past week she'd done internet research that told her the kick would push the gun up. He was firing, too, but her focus narrowed to *him* in an instant of surreal clarity. When she pulled the trigger, the recoil was greater than she'd anticipated, but she'd hit him. He slumped, hanging out the car window. The gun he'd held fell.

Something stung Maddy's arm. Had she been shot? But who—

There. The driver of that same taxi had opened his door and was firing over the roof. Afraid she'd miss and hit someone in a passing car or on the opposite sidewalk, she hesitated.

Behind her at least two voices yelled, "Put the gun down! Put the gun down!"

Guards? Would they shoot *her*? She flung herself flat, cheek pressed to the gritty concrete. A man crawled over her and, panicked, she started to scramble away.

"Maddy, it's me!"

Ruzinski. Thank God he wasn't dead, although blood darkened his raincoat and dripped onto her.

She heard more gunshots but had no idea who was shooting now.

Will. Oh, dear Lord, was he dead? Terrified, she knew *he* would have thrown himself over her if he wasn't badly injured, at least.

"Put the gun down!" a man yelled right above her. She saw the blue-uniform-clad legs. A police officer.

Suddenly, her hands trembled viciously. Another hand closed over hers and gently removed the gun, laying it on the pavement. A foot in a shiny black shoe appeared in her limited vision and edged the weapon out of reach.

She closed her eyes, gripped by shock. But... "Will," she mumbled.

Ruzinski rolled off her. He was swearing, a litany that seemed to punctuate the moment.

Somewhere, a woman still screamed. Somebody else was sobbing. Sirens screamed, too.

Maddy had to know. Cradling her injured arm, she awkwardly pushed herself to her knees. She must have skinned them, because they burned fiercely. She rose until she was kneeling and could turn in place.

Will.

There he was, a few feet away. Dead or only unconscious. She crawled to him. He lay on his back, his face slack.

"Will," she whimpered. "Will, open your eyes."

She wrenched open his raincoat but didn't find any blood. A pulse throbbed in his neck and he was breathing.

"Ma'am, out of the way," a man said. Wearing a uniform, he crouched to assess Will's condition. A paramedic, whose sharp eyes lifted to her. "You're injured, too."

She shook her head. "I'm just scraped up."

"You have blood all over your raincoat."

Maddy looked down. "Oh. No, that's from him." She gestured. "He's a US marshal."

The man yelled, "Higley, over here!"

Within seconds he slid a brace around Will's neck and he and a second paramedic, a woman, shifted Will onto a stretcher. Moving fast, they lifted him and started toward an aide car.

"Wait!" Maddy tried to stand. "I need to—"

"Ma'am, let me check you over." Another uniformed woman with kind eyes reached for the buttons on Maddy's raincoat.

Two others worked over Ruzinski. Face creased with pain, he rolled his head toward her. "You okay?"

"Yes. I think so." Actually, she hurt a whole lot, but that was because her battered body had once again been assaulted.

"Then get inside and do what you came to do. Put that scumbag away," he said fiercely.

The ambulance with Will inside pulled away from the curb. Maddy wanted desperately to run after it, but Ruzinski was right. This had all been about keeping her from testifying.

The closest EMT helped her to her feet. "You're in pain. You need to go to the hospital. Here. You can ride with—"

"No." She pulled away. "I'm a witness in a trial. I have to get inside. All I need is to clean up."

"I'm sure your testimony can be pushed back…"

"Then we'd have this to do again." She fully looked around for the first time. Ruzinski was now being loaded into another ambulance. A bloodstain marked where the woman had been shot and fallen. Other people sat, faces gray with shock as paramedics worked over them. Handbags, briefcases, coats, umbrellas and women's scarves littered the sidewalk, abandoned where they'd fallen. Police cars and ambulances jammed the street, so many lights flashing Maddy's eyes were dazzled. More cops than she'd ever seen at one time interviewed stunned people who were lucky enough to be uninjured.

The Uber driver who'd delivered her and Will was one of those. Even as he talked, his head swung toward her and their gazes met. She wanted to say *I'm sorry, we used you*, but at least he was unhurt.

Just once she looked at the body half hanging out of the taxi. The man she had killed.

Then she asked the EMT beside her, "Will you help me?" She began hobbling toward the entrance.

"Ma'am, you should—" He gave up and put a hand under her elbow to support her. Once she was inside, Maddy thanked him and groped in her pocket for the latest phone Will had given her.

Before she had a chance to dial, a woman emerged from an elevator. Gaze intense, she hurried toward Maddy.

"WELL." HEAD TILTED to one side, Cynthia Yates assessed Maddy. "That's an improvement."

They were in a restroom on the same floor as the designated courtroom. On a first-name basis now, they'd been in here for half an hour, delayed because once Maddy gingerly removed the dirty, bloody raincoat, balled it up and shoved it into the trash, she realized a bullet had grazed her upper arm. That was what had stung.

While Cynthia disappeared in search of a first-aid kit, Maddy managed one-handed to peel off ruined tights and the bloody, ripped blouse, then washed her scraped knees and hands. Then she washed the stage makeup from her face, leaving it stark.

After returning with supplies, Cynthia applied copious antibiotic ointment to the ugly graze and then wrapped Maddy's arm with gauze. More ointment on her raw palms, more gauze. Maddy winced as she donned a borrowed white blouse and tights. She let the DA brush her hair and apply light makeup.

Supporting her broken arm with her opposite hand, Maddy grimaced. "I don't know what happened to my sling."

"How about some more gauze?" the other woman suggested, brandishing the roll.

"I'm starting to look like a mummy, but why not?"

"Not a mummy, a zombie."

She would have laughed if the ache of fear hadn't held her in such a tight grip. Why hadn't somebody called to tell her about Will's condition? Ruzinski... well, he might be in surgery, she realized.

"I think this is as good as it's going to get," she said, studying herself in the mirror. Aside from her eyes, she looked fine. Good, really, now that the bruises were gone. Only her eyes betrayed the craziness inside her, the shock and fear and anger.

Cynthia's phone buzzed. She glanced at it. "Good timing. We're ready for you."

Maddy closed her eyes, drew a few deep breaths and sought composure. So many people had sacrificed so she could do this. She wouldn't let them down.

The restroom door had just closed behind them when her phone rang. Maddy snatched it from her pocket and answered.

"Will?"

"Yeah." His voice sounded as if it had been scraped over gravel, but was so welcome. "You okay?"

Maddy blinked back tears. "Basically. What about you?"

"The vest stopped a few bullets. I have a cracked sternum and cracked or broken ribs. Mostly, I knocked myself out when I went down. They won't let me go yet." He paused. "I'm sorry. I wanted to be there for you."

"Oh, Will." She stopped in the hall and turned

away from the prosecutor. "I made it here only because of you. This part, I know how to do."

"I guess you do."

Behind her, Cynthia said, "Maddy, we need to
go."

"Kick butt, sweetheart," Will said. "As soon as I
can break out of here, I'll come get you."

"Okay." *I love you.* But she had no idea whether
he'd want to hear those words.

The hall had emptied while they were closeted
in the restroom. The click of their heels seemed to
echo.

A guard opened the heavy wooden door for them
to enter. People in the galley automatically turned
to see who was coming in. Attorneys on both sides
did the same.

No, they weren't all attorneys. The man she'd seen
murder her client had turned, too, to see her stride
in, his face frozen with shock.

Surprise!

WILL GAVE SERIOUS thought to getting dressed and
walking out. Not like anybody could stop him.

Impatience eating at him, he waited, though. He'd
had an MRI and wanted to hear what, if anything,
they'd seen. Brain damage wouldn't help him get accepted to medical school. The last time he'd pushed
the little button to summon a nurse, she patted his
hand and said, "Just a few more minutes."

Damn, he'd wanted to see Maddy on the stand,
staring that son of a bitch in the eye.

There wasn't any way someone could have smuggled a gun to the defendant, was there?

No. Besides, after the scene outside, the bailiff and every armed officer in the courtroom would be hyperalert.

He had to quit worrying…but where in *hell* was the doctor?

THE COURTROOM LOOKED different from this perspective. *Get used to it*, Maddy told herself. After all, there was another trial to come.

Any other time, she might have been nervous, but anger was her predominant emotion. A few weeks ago, seeing Kevin Mooney's face might have rattled her. What she saw him do was terrible beyond any other experience in her life. But hey, now she'd experienced plenty of other violence. All, of course, because of what she saw that day.

Defensive counsel, a man Maddy didn't know, objected to the sling she wore. "If she's attempting to draw sympathy…"

A gleam of delight lit in Cynthia's eyes. "Your honor, we're certainly prepared to explain how Ms. Kane came to be injured."

The judge tipped her head to study the attorney. "You'll have your chance to ask questions. I'll allow it if you choose to pursue that line of inquiry."

Cynthia calmly led Maddy through the day she'd witnessed a murder. The second best moment came when Cynthia asked, "Do you see that man in the courtroom today?"

"Yes." Maddy pointed. "Right there."

The best moment? When she was asked if the gunman had spoken. Maddy said firmly, "Yes, he did. Ms. Bessey was begging. She wanted to know why he was going to kill her. His exact words were, 'You're a problem for Brian Torkelson.'" The courtroom was utterly silent during her pause. "Then he shot her."

The opposing counsel's attempt to shake her went nowhere. Her previous courtroom experience gave her the confidence to take her time before answering questions, ensuring that she spoke clearly with no digressions that could weaken her testimony.

Somehow it was no surprise that he didn't raise the subject of her sling. He might not know about the bomb or the ambush in Bellevue that left an FBI agent badly injured. She'd prefer to think he didn't. However, she'd seen a woman hustle into the courtroom to pass a note to him, likely informing him about what had taken place out front only an hour ago. He couldn't risk letting the jury hear about it.

The judge thanked her for her testimony and Maddy rose, surprised to find that her legs weren't entirely steady. Unwilling to meet her eyes, the defendant stared down at papers on the table in front of him.

Maddy walked out.

THE RELIEF ON Maddy's face when she saw him loosened the knot in Will's chest.

He hadn't been happy to spot her standing alone in

the lobby. What were these people thinking? But as he strode toward her, a guard materialized to intercept him, backing off only when she said his name and rushed forward.

He didn't care where they were. He pulled her into his arms, his kiss fueled by all the tumult the day had set loose in his chest. He needed to know she really was all right. This was the only way he could reassure himself.

He did hold on to enough awareness of his surroundings to know they had to get out of here before this could go any further. Also, he had to deliver one piece of irritating news.

He gave their pulses time to slow before he said, "I've been asked to bring you to the police station. They need to interview you."

She gripped his hand. "You'll stay with me?"

"I'm going to guess they won't let me sit in on the interview, but I'll be waiting."

"Um…how did you get here?"

Will grinned. "I went for variety and hired a taxi."

Maddy laughed. "Just think, what if the same Uber driver had come to pick you up?"

"If I were him, I'd be taking the rest of the day off."

She made a face. "I'd suggest *we* do, except by the time we get home it'll be evening." Her expression changed. "That is… I guess I shouldn't assume I can keep imposing on you—"

Will scowled. "Of course you're coming home with me."

Did his cabin feel like home to her? Man, he wanted to think so.

Not the moment to have that talk, he reminded himself.

Fortunately, the Seattle PD detective who interviewed Maddy knew the backstory and, after hearing her side of what happened upon their arrival at the courthouse, assured her there'd be no repercussions for shooting a man who'd clearly been trying to kill her.

During the taxi ride back to Northgate, where Will had left his Jeep, Maddy told him the detective had congratulated her on her skill with a handgun. She smiled impishly. "I shook him up a little when I told him I've never fired one before."

Once they'd been dropped by his Jeep, parked in the transit lot at Northgate, Maddy insisted on driving.

"I'm fine," he said automatically. "Your arm is in a sling."

A steely look in her eyes, she held out her hand for the keys. "If your Jeep had a manual transmission, that might be a problem. As it is, I can drive with one hand. You, though… Major narcotics? Head injury? MRI? You were *unconscious*, Will."

Feeling chagrined, he dropped the keys into her hand.

Once on their way, she asked about Ruzinski and any other victims from this morning. "I saw that woman with blood all over her chest."

"She went straight into surgery and is still in critical condition. Two other bystanders are, too, not to mention the injured from the decoy team." He hesitated. "Including your replacement. A bullet grazed her head, but she'll be okay."

Maddy absorbed that. So many people, injured and dead, to keep her silent.

"I saw Ruzinski in recovery before I left," Will added, "and he asked about you. His wife and an adult son were there by then. The surgeon told us he expects a complete recovery."

"So nobody died."

"Two of the bad guys are dead, one also in critical condition."

Her fingers tightened on the steering wheel. "Which one lived?"

"The one I shot. He posed as a homeless wino."

"Oh. I saw him when we got out of the taxi."

"He's the first one who started shooting. Goes without saying that the detectives and FBI agents who showed up at the hospital really want him to survive. One more nail in Torkelson's coffin."

"This guy might not know who had hired them."

"Possible, but we can hope. Now, tell me how it went in court."

She did.

"Too bad the guy didn't ask you about the broken arm."

Maddy laughed again. "Cynthia was hopeful, but I think by then he'd heard about the shoot-out in front of the courthouse."

A phone rang. He immediately identified it as the one she had been carrying. Since she didn't have a spare hand, Will answered.

"Mr. Gannon?" It was Yates herself. She asked to speak to Maddy, and when he explained that she was driving with only one usable hand, she said, "I have good news. During a recess Mr. Mooney's attorney approached us. He's willing to accept a plea in exchange for us taking the death penalty off the table. He'll go for a life sentence with a possibility of parole. In return, he'll testify against Torkelson."

Will grasped the consequences immediately. "Eliminating Maddy won't save him anymore."

"Unless Mr. Mooney were to be killed, but we're asking for solitary confinement until Torkelson is convicted."

"That's excellent news."

He repeated what she'd said aloud for Maddy's benefit.

"Oh." She went quiet for a minute. "He won't dare go to trial now. Everything would come out. The bomb on the plane that resulted in a US marshal's death, the men who tried to hunt us down, the assault intended to prevent me meeting with Yates, and the last-ditch attempt today. He'll go for a plea."

"Don't suppose he'll fare well in prison," Will said with satisfaction.

"No. It's all over."

She didn't seem to want to talk after that. What could he do but let her have the space she needed to come to terms with what had to be an emotional crash after a year of unstoppable tension? The news was good, but still unsettling.

She'd want to go home, he realized. Her parents would need to see her. After today's spectacular events, her law firm was sure to welcome her back with open arms.

Will's mood plummeted as the miles passed.

SHE DIDN'T NEED him anymore. The realization shocked Maddy. Perhaps she should be glad, and she was in one way; if they had any kind of future, it had to be as equals. In another way…she hadn't expected the end to come so abruptly.

It wasn't a sure thing that Torkelson would take a plea…except she knew it was. He'd be foolish to risk a trial, and that was one thing he wasn't.

Maddy had expected to have more time with Will. More idea of how he felt about her.

When they let themselves into his cabin, she sneaked a sidelong look at him to see that some of the creases in his face had deepened. He might just be preoccupied, she decided, but what was he thinking about? Getting his life back?

"I can hardly wait to get out of these clothes," she said. He only watched as she scooped undergarments, shorts, T-shirt and flip-flops from the small pile of her belongings.

She shut herself in the bathroom and changed, her mind on him the whole time.

Talk to him? Wait until he said something? Cheerily announce there was no reason she couldn't go stay with her parents now?

Maddy felt sick when she emerged from the bathroom.

Will stood right where she'd left him. "I'll miss you," he said.

She bit her lip and nodded. He looked so much like he had that first day, when he'd come upon her. *Déjà vu*, she thought. "This feels—"

"I don't want you to go," he said gruffly. "I know you're probably eager to get back to work, but... maybe we could figure something out."

Her eyes stung. She started forward, wanting his arms around her, but she remembered all those cracked or broken bones and stopped.

"I don't want to go," she admitted. "I've been hoping—"

"God." Two long strides, and he swept her into an embrace. "Damn, Maddy. The whole way back all I could think was you'd be in a hurry to go home."

She lifted her head to smile shakily. "You know I haven't lived with my parents for a very long time. And my apartment was never exactly home." She swallowed. "You are."

He kissed her almost clumsily, desperation allowing for no gentle preliminaries. Maddy held on as tightly, tangled her tongue with his, nipped his lip, wrapped a leg around his. Oblivious to their surroundings and the fact that they were clothed, she tried to pull him closer. She needed him inside her. *Now.*

They stripped each other. He was sane enough to don a condom before they made hard, frantic love on the sofa. Maddy wasn't sure she'd have noticed if he hadn't.

They ended with her sprawled atop him, her arm in the way, of course. She lay savoring the long, muscular body near hers, the gradually slowing beat of his heart. The groan when she shifted her weight.

Horrified that she'd let herself forget his injuries, she tried to lift herself off him, but Will held her in place.

Finally, she whispered, "I was afraid you still thought you weren't good enough for me."

He groaned again. Before she could worry, he said, "We need to buy a new sofa."

Maddy burst out laughing. "That's one of the few really great pieces of furniture I have."

"Good," he said, a smile in his voice. His hand slid down her back, his fingers delicately exploring her string of vertebrae. "We need to talk about how we can make this work."

"I suppose."

They got dressed and jointly started dinner, since there wasn't much she could do with only one hand. She did most of the talking, telling him she didn't want to go back to work at the same firm, and maybe not at all as a defense attorney. "I think I'd like to become a prosecutor. Everything that's happened has changed my perspective. Not just that. It's changed *me*."

The knife he'd been using to dice a bell pepper

still in hand, he kissed her lightly. "Meeting you has changed me."

Neither of them said *I love you*. They didn't have to. She knew, and thought he did, and really, what was the hurry?

"You'll come with me to meet my parents?" she asked. Seeing his expression, she added, "They'll like you. I promise."

He had her when he said, voice rough, "Maybe we can take a week or two to go to Lake Shasta, too. Meet my dad. And did I ever tell you I worked one summer for a place that rents houseboats? We could do that."

"Yes." What could be more perfect than a week on the water, just the two of them? She held up her hand, forefinger and thumb almost touching. "First time I set eyes on you? I was *this* close to just shooting you, you know."

He only laughed. "And I was so sure you couldn't hit me if you tried."

Maddy raised her eyebrows. "Now you know not to underestimate me."

Smiling, Will laid down the knife and used both hands to cradle her face. "Never," he murmured. "That's one mistake I'll never make."

* * * * *

YOU HAVE
JUST READ A
HARLEQUIN®
INTRIGUE®
BOOK

If you were **captivated** by the **gripping, page-turning romantic suspense,** be sure to look for all six Harlequin® Intrigue® books every month.

AVAILABLE THIS MONTH FROM
Harlequin Intrigue®

A THREAT TO HIS FAMILY
Longview Ridge Ranch • by Delores Fossen

When threatened by an unknown assailant, single dad Deputy Owen Slater must protect his daughter with the help of PI Laney Martin, who is investigating her sister's murder. Can they find out who is after them before someone else is killed?

TACTICAL FORCE
Declan's Defenders • by Elle James

Former marine and Declan's Defenders member Jack Snow and White House staffer Anne Bellamy must work together to stop an assassin from killing the president of the United States. But when their search makes Anne the killer's target, can they track down the criminal before he finds them?

CODE CONSPIRACY
Red, White and Built: Delta Force Deliverance
by Carol Ericson

When Gray Prescott's Delta Force commander goes AWOL under suspicious circumstances, he turns to his ex, computer hacker extraordinaire Jerrica West, for answers. But what they find might be deadly...

DEADLY COVER-UP
Fortress Defense • by Julie Anne Lindsey

With the help of bodyguard Wyatt Stone, newly single mother Violet Ames races to discover the truth about her grandmother's near-fatal accident. Before long, she'll learn that incident is part of a conspiracy long protected by a powerful local family.

BRACE FOR IMPACT
by Janice Kay Johnson

Maddy Kane is a key witness in a high-profile murder case, and her only chance at survival lies in the hands of former army medic Will Gannon. With armed goons hot on their trail, can they survive long enough for Maddy to testify?

IN HIS SIGHTS
Stealth • by Danica Winters

Jarrod Martin's investigation into a crime syndicate takes an unexpected turn when he joins forces with criminal heiress Mindy Kohl to protect her five-year-old niece from ruthless killers.

LOOK FOR THESE AND OTHER HARLEQUIN INTRIGUE BOOKS WHEREVER BOOKS ARE SOLD, INCLUDING MOST BOOKSTORES, SUPERMARKETS, DISCOUNT STORES AND DRUGSTORES.

HIATMBPA0120

COMING NEXT MONTH FROM

(H) HARLEQUIN

INTRIGUE

Available January 21, 2020

#1905 WITNESS PROTECTION WIDOW
A Winchester, Tennessee Thriller • by Debra Webb
In witness protection under a new name, Allison James, aka the Widow, must work together with her ex-boyfriend, US Marshal Jaxson Stevens, to outsmart her deceased husband's powerful crime family and bring justice to the group.

#1906 DISRUPTIVE FORCE
A Declan's Defenders Novel • by Elle James
Assassin CJ Grainger has insider knowledge about the terrorist organization Trinity after escaping the group. With help from Cole McCastlain, a member of Declan's Defenders, can she stop Trinity before its plan to murder government officials is executed?

#1907 CONFLICTING EVIDENCE
The Mighty McKenzies Series • by Lena Diaz
Peyton Sterling knows she can only prove her brother's innocence by working with US Marshal Colin McKenzie, even though he helped put her brother in jail. Yet in their search for the truth, they'll unearth secrets that are more dangerous than they could have imagined...

#1908 MISSING IN THE MOUNTAINS
A Fortress Defense Case • by Julie Anne Lindsey
Emma Hart knows her ex-boyfriend's security firm is the only group she can trust to help her find her abducted sister. But she's shocked when her ex, Sawyer Lance, is the one who comes to her aid.

#1909 HER ASSASSIN FOR HIRE
A Stealth Novel • by Danica Winters
When Zoey Martin's brother goes missing, she asks her ex, black ops assassin Eli Wayne, for help. With a multimillion-dollar bounty on Zoey's brother's head, they won't be the only ones looking for him, and some people would kill for that much money...

#1910 THE FINAL SECRET
by Cassie Miles
On her first assignment as a bodyguard for ARC Security, former army corps member Genevieve "Gennie" Fox and her boss, former SEAL Noah Sheridan, must solve the murder he has been framed for.

YOU CAN FIND MORE INFORMATION ON UPCOMING HARLEQUIN TITLES, FREE EXCERPTS AND MORE AT HARLEQUIN.COM.

HICNM0120

Four Days Until Trial

Sunday, February 2
Winchester, Tennessee
It was colder now.

The meteorologist had warned that it might snow on
Monday. The temperature was already dropping. She
didn't mind. She had no appointments, no deadlines and
no place to be—except *here*.

Four days.

Four more days until *the* day.

If she lived that long.

She stopped and surveyed the thick woods around her,
making a full three-sixty turn. Nothing but trees and this
one trail for as far as the eye could see. The fading sun
trickled through the bare limbs. This place had taken her
through the last of summer and then fall, and now winter
was nearing an end. In all that time she had seen only

one other living human. It was best, they said. For her protection, they insisted.

It was true. But she had never felt more alone in her life.

Bob nudged her. She pushed aside the troubling thoughts and looked down at her black Labrador. "I know, boy. I should get moving. It's cold out here."

Allowing herself to get caught out in the woods in the dark—no matter that she knew the way back to the cabin by heart—was a bad idea. She started forward once more. Her hiking boots crunched on the rocks and the few frozen leaves scattered across the trail. Bob trotted beside her, his tail wagging happily. She'd never had a dog before coming to this place. Growing up, her mother's allergies hadn't allowed pets. Later, when she was out on her own, the apartment building hadn't permitted pets.

Even after she married and moved into one of Atlanta's megamansions, she couldn't have a dog. Her husband had hated dogs, cats, any sort of pet. How had she not recognized the evil in him then? Anyone who hated animals so much couldn't be good.

She hugged herself, rubbed her arms. Thinking of him, even in such simple terms, unsettled her. Soon she hoped she would be able to put that part of her life behind her and never look back again.

Never, ever.

"Not soon enough," she muttered.

Don't miss
Witness Protection Widow *by Debra Webb,*
available February 2020 wherever
Harlequin Intrigue books and ebooks are sold.

Harlequin.com

HIEXP0120